Nietzsche's Notebook of 1887-1888

Friedrich Nietzsche

GRAPEVINE INDIA

Published by

GRAPEVINE INDIA PUBLISHERS PVT LTD

www.grapevineindia.com
Delhi | Mumbai
email: grapevineindiapublishers@gmail.com

Ordering Information:
Quantity sales: Special discounts are available on quantity
purchases by corporations, associations, and others.
For details, reach out to the publisher.

First published by Grapevine India 2023

[11 = W II 3 November 1887 - March 1888]

Nice 24 November 1887 (Nizza den 24. November 1887)

11 [1]

We should want nothing of what you cannot. Ask yourself, will you go ahead? Or will you go for you? In the first case is one, at best, a shepherd, that is no demands of (Nothbedarf) the herd. In another case, one may little differently (Andrs), -- of the for-itself-to-go-can (von sich Für-sich-gehn-können), one must go otherwise and elsewhere-- can. In both cases, it can and can the one, do not you want the otherwise (Andre)

11 [2]

With people for love take and keep his heart open house: that is liberal, but not refined. You can see the hearts that are capable of making hospitality at the many curtained windows and closed shutters: they keep their best rooms empty to say the least, they expect guests with whom you do not for love (furlieb) takes...

11 [3]

One is at the cost of artists that you what to call all non-artists "form", as content, as "the thing itself" feels. So of course you belong to a world turned upside down, for now one of the content becomes something merely formal - our life included.

11 [4]

A letter reminds me of German youths, horned Siegfried and other Wagnerian. All respect for the German-sufficiency! There are modest intelligences in northern Germany, where even the intelligence of the cross does enough (genugthut) newspaper. Outstanding one could sometimes get the suspicion that the young nation (Reich), in its voracious appetite for all kinds of colonies and Africa, which owns the earth, has not suddenly swallowed the two famous black-brown islands, Borneo and Horneo...

11 [5]

If you are a philosopher, as it was always a philosopher, one has no eye for what was and what is - you only see what (Seiende) is. But since there is nothing being (Seiende), so there was the philosopher saved only the imaginary, as his "world".

11 [6]

It goes to reason if you always on the reasons go.

11 [7]

Apply a bead between two springs, which already grows a little wing:

11 [8]

"A drive for the better (Besseren)" - formula for "go to the toilet"

11 [9]

Sainte-Beuve: Nothing from man, full of a hypocritical hatred of all men spirits: defamatory wanders around, cowardly, bored, curious, - a wenches basically, with a wife-revenge and female sensuality (- the latter holds him close set of monasteries and other breeding grounds of mysticism, at times even in the vicinity of Saint-Simon) By the way, a real genius of slander, inexhaustibly rich in resources to able for example to a deadly manner praise, not without a pleasing virtuoso alacrity, his to make art on display, where there is some out of place: namely, from all kinds of audiences, the fear of something is. Of course he takes after her also to his listeners with her revenge, secretly, petty, unclean, in its particularity, it must pay all unavoidable noble natures, that they have reverence for himself, - he has not! even the male, pride, whole, self-certain appeals to him, shakes him up to the riot. - This is now the psychologist comme il faut, namely according to the measure and the necessity of the present esprit francais, the so late, so sick, so curious, so driven from listening (aushorcherisch) so lascivious as he; secretive sniffling as he, instinctively made the acquaintance with people from the bottom and behind (Hintenher) searching, not much different than the dogs do it among themselves (which are also on their way psychologists). Basically with the plebeian instincts and Rousseau used: hence romantics - because romanticism grunts among all the mob and is hungry for "nobility"; revolutionary, but passable by the fear still held in check. Without freedom from everything which has power (public opinion, academy, court, even Port-Royal). His tired in the last analysis, at times even without belief in its right to be there, a spirit that has been wasted from an early age, which is wasted feeling that is itself becoming thinner and older. The last living still continue from one day to another, from mere cowardice; the embittered against everything great in person and thing, against all that which believes in itself, as it is, unfortunately, poet and half-women (Halbweib) enough to have as great power to feel, the curves resistant, like the famous worm because it is constantly feeling of something large came. As a critic, without measure rod, spin and stop, with the tongue of the cosmopolitan libertine for many things, but without the courage even to be somewhat more unusual libertinage, thus subjecting an undetermined classicism itself. As a historian, without philosophy, and the power of the gaze, instinctively, the task of teaching in all the main things negative and the mask of objectivity hold (- so that one of the worst patterns, the last, France has had): apart as cheap, little of the things, where a fine and uses up flavor is the highest authority, and where he really the courage to be oneself, the desire has in himself (- in this he is akin to the Parnassian, like him, the represent most refined and most vain form of modern self-loathing, self-emptying). "Sainte-Beuve vu une fois le-a premier Empereur. C'etait a Boulogne: il etait en train de pisser. N'est-ce pas dans cette posture un peu-la, et qu'il a vu depuis juge tous les grands hommes "(Journal des Goncourt, 2, p. 239) - to tell of his evil enemies, the Goncourt.

11 [10]

Types of decadence.

The Romantics

The "free spirits" Sainte-Beuve The actor.

The nihilists.

The artistes.

The brutalist.

The delicious.

11 [11]

En amour, la seule victoire est la fuite. - Napoleon.

11 [12]

canis reversus ad vomitum suum

11 [13]

Ne sont pas les philosophes faits pour s'aimer. Ne les aigles volente point en compagnie. Il faut laisser cela perdrix aux, aux... etourneaux planner audessus et avoir of the handle, voila le grands lot of geniuses. - Galiani.

11 [14]

Le hasard, pere de la fortune et souvent beau-pere de la vertu. - Galiani.

11 [15]

(Ni Tamour ni les dieux; ce double mal nous tue. Sully Prudhomme.)

11 [16]

Behind all this moral scribbling rural female, of G. Eliot, I always hear the excited voice of all literary debutante: "je me verrai, je me lirai, depending m'extasierai et dirai ever: Possible, que eu tant d'esprit j'aie?.."

11[17]

vomitus matutinus of newspapers

11 [18]

hortum si cum bibliotheca Habe, nihil deerit. Cicero.

11 [19]

Notum quid foemina furens. Virg. Aen. V. 6

11 [20]

"Mieux vaut un monstre gai <qu'un sentimental ennuyeux>"

11 [21]

come l'uom s'eterna (Inf. XV, 85)

11 [22]

"Yo me sucedo a mi mismo," I say like that old man in Lope de Vega, smiling, as he did: for I know it absolutely cannot remember how old I am already, and how young I'll still be...

11[23]

- we also have plenty of reasons to be happy and even grateful to have, if only in the way it was that old joker, the re bene gesta tamquam of an amorous tryst returned home. Ut disinterest vires, he said to himself with the meekness of a saint, tamen est laudanda voluptas.

11 [24]

George Sand. I read the first Lettres d'un voyageur: like everything that comes from Rousseau, false, from the ground up, hypocritical moralistic, like herself, this "artist". I consider this colorful wallpaper-style is not, nor is this excited mob-ambition to "make" passions, heroic attitudes and thoughts that seem like attitudes. How cold she must have been there - cold, like Victor Hugo, like Balzac, like all true romantics: - and how smug she might thereby have been lying, this broad fertile cow, which some German had on him, like Rousseau himself, and in any case at the end of all French taste and wit only possible... But is Ernest Renan was they worshiped...

11 [25]

People, the fates are those that carry by themselves, bear stories, all the kind of heroic carrier: oh, how happy they even want to take a rest by himself! as they thirst after heavy heart and neck to be going for hours at least, what it expresses! And how vain they thirst... wait, they look at everything that passes, no one comes to meet them with only the thousandth of suffering and passion, no one guesses,! how they are waiting... Finally, finally, they learn their first life-wisdom - not to wait longer, and then immediately had it's second: to be sociable, to be humble, to endure from now on everyone to endure every kind - in short, a little more wear than they have been worn...

11 [26]

- and if the math without prejudice, the conditions under which any one here on earth, perfection is achieved, which will not escape, how much whimsical and embarrassing these conditions belongs. It seems that at every major growth dung and manure of any kind does needful. To take a paradoxical case, he claimed with respect to the perfection of the modern woman with an authority that is responsible for this delicate point is not to be underestimated, perhaps, the due de Morny, this experienced and "experienced" women's expert on the last of France, that it even could serve a vice, namely the tribaderie: "la femme qui paraffins, la parfait, l'accompli."

Nice 25 November 1887.

11[27]

Have a wife, Cosima Wagner is the only woman a larger scale, I know, but I expect it to her, to Wagner that has she spoiled. How did it happen? He "earned" such a woman is not: thanks to fell it to her. - The W Parsifal was first and foremost and beginners a taste condescension W s to the Catholic instincts of his wife, the daughter of Liszt's, a kind of gratitude and humility on the part of a much simpler weaker creature whose suffering up to a which protect and encourage understanding, that is, to a stronger, more narrow-minded - even a last act of that eternal cowardice of the man above all "eternal feminine." - Whether not all great artists so far by adoring women have been spoiled? If this nonsense, vain and sensual monkeys - because they are together with all (allesammt) almost - for the first time and very close to idol worship experience, the means to drive the woman in such cases, with its lowest and highest desires, then it comes soon enough to end: the last remnant of criticism, self-loathing, shame and humility before the larger is gone - from then on they are all degenerate capable. - To despise these artists, who in the bitterest and strongest period of their development are reasons enough, their supporters in the lump, this silence has become artists are inevitably the victims of every first intelligent love (- or rather, every woman who is intelligent enough in terms of the artist's most personal intelligently give him "understand" as suffering him to "love"...)

11 [28]

The woman who does not deserve it forfeited, the husband (Mann)

The woman, bom as an idolater perishes, the idols - the husband (Gatten).

11 [29]

You can do that, what is the reason that it gives any development does not find itself in the way of research on development, you will not want to understand it as "becoming", became even less than... become the "will to power" cannot be

11 [30]

A bird's eye level and win considering where we can understand how to put things back how it should go even really about: like any kind of "imperfection" and the suffering with their into the highest desirability is...

11 [31]

Overall vision of the future European: the same as the most intelligent animal slaves, very hardworking, basically very humble, curious to excess, often, spoiled, weakwilled - a cosmopolitan and emotional intelligences chaos. As would be made him a stronger stand out style? With such a classic taste? The classic taste: this is the will to simplify, strengthen, to the visibility of happiness to horror, the courage to psychological nakedness (- simplification is a consequence of the will to step up, the appearance of letting the happiness similarly, the nudity, a consequence of the will the horror...) To get out of that chaos to this design to fight rising (emporzukampfen) - it requires a necessity: one must have a choice, either to perish or to prevail. A majestic breed can grow up only by the horrific and violent beginnings. Problem: where are the barbarians of the 20th Century? Apparently they are visible only after tremendous socialist crises and consolidate (consolidiren), - it will be the elements that the greatest hardness against themselves and are capable longest will all guarantee can...

11 [32]

On the psychology of the "shepherds". The great moderate (Durchschnittlichen).

Can you hide, that a mind and taste average must be to leave deep wide popular effects, and that as there are still not allowed to be taken to dishonor Voltaire, when he Abbe Trublet with very best rights "la perfection de la mediocriter" has called? (- He would not to say, that he would be one exception was, like the Neapolitan Galiani was an exception, those deepest and most thoughtful buffoon who has brought forth that cheerful century, whence then its power lead where his superiority over his time?) One way might even say the same thing in regard to a lot of popular case also the founder of Christianity must be something of a "perfection de la mediocriter" been. But once you leave the main principles of the gospel of the famous Sermon on the Mount to a person consolidate (concresciren): - you will afterwards also be no longer in doubt, just why such a shepherd and mountain preacher seductive to all kind of herd has worked.

11 [33]

- "Une croyance presque que c'est tout instinctive chez moi quand il parle ment puissant homme et a plus forte raison quand il ecrit." - Stendhal.

11 [34]

Flaubert was neither made nor Stendhal, Merimee, and one could make him furious when "Monsieur Beyle," quoted in his presence. The difference is: Beyle comes from Voltaire, Flaubert, Victor Hugo.

The "men of 1830" (- men...?) Have an absurd idolatry with the love with Alfred de Musset, Richard Wagner, also of debauchery and vice (Ausschweifung und dem Laste)...

"Je suis de 1830, moi! Apprise j'ai a lire dans Hernani, et j'aurai voulu etre Lara! J'execre toutes les contemporaines laugh, l'ordinaire de l'existence et l'ignominie of bonheurs faciles." Flaubert.

11 [35]

The sexuality (Geschlechtlichkeit), the ambition, the desire to slip on and cheating, the great joyous gratitude for life and its typical conditions - this is essential and the pagan cult has good conscience on its side. - The unnaturalness (already in ancient Greek) is fighting against the heathen, as morality, dialectic.

Nice 15 December 1887

11 [36]

On the rank decides the quantum of power that you are, the rest is cowardice.

11 [37]

Whose instinct is to rank order from one who hates the between educated (Zwischengebilde) and between images (Zwischenbildner): everything medium is his enemy.

11 [38]

From the pressure of wealth, from the tension of forces that are constantly growing in us and have no clue to discharge, is a state, as it goes before a storm: the nature that we are darkened itself. This too is pessimism... One lesson that such a state makes an end, by any thing commanded, a revaluation of values by virtue of which the accumulated forces a way, a where it is shown so that they explode in flashes and deeds needs absolutely no chance to be teaching: by throwing force, which was crowded (zusammengedrangt) and jammed to agony, it brings good luck.

11 [39]

- with whom I have little sympathy. I reckon they are crustaceans. In the first place: if one meddles with them so they pubs, and then - they're going backwards.

11 [40]

- fresh milk heart (— kuhwarme Milchherzen)

11 [41]

A weary traveler, to receive the harsh barking of a dog.

11 [42]

- a runaway, who was long in prison, in fear of a jailer: now he is afraid of its path, the shadow of a stick makes him even stumble.

11[43]

- Virtue in Renaissance style, virtu, virtue moraline

11 [44]

That one's life, his health, his honor at risk that is the result of wantonness and an overflowing wasteful will: not out of philanthropy, but because every great danger our curiosity with respect to the measure of our strength, of our courage to challenge.

11[45]

Emerson, much more enlightened, much simpler, refined, fortunately, one entitled to instinctively feed on ambrosia and leaves behind the indigestible in things. Carlyle, who loved him very much, said of him anyway, "he gives us enough not to bite whatever may be said with truth, but not to the detriment of Emerson's.

Carlyle, a man of strong words and attitudes of eccentricity, a rhetorician of distress, the resistant strong (agacirt) desire for a faith and a sense of inability to do so imprecisely so that a typical romantic -) The desire for a strong faith is not the evidence of a strong faith, rather the contrary: it has one, then the just betrays the fact that you have the luxury of skepticism and incredulity of the frivolous may indulge, - one is just rich enough to do so. Carlyle in a little stunned by the vehemence of his admiration for people of strong faith and his rage against all less simple-minded: this constant passionate dishonesty against him, to speak morally disgusted me about him. That the English just admire him for his honesty, that is English, and, given that they are the people of the perfect cannot, even cheap, and not only understandable. Carlyle is basically an atheist who wants to be.

11 [46]

In these contentious essays in which I my campaign against the fatal current value-judgment, to our overestimation of morality would continue

Such a word of peace is as cheap at the end of this war treatises (kriegerischen Abhandlungen), which I think our campaign against one fateful judgments of value, from our previous estimate and overestimation of morality have opened.

11[47]

- Humidity and other ideals thawing wind

11 [48]

Would not say which is meant that he also seems: a spirit who wants the big and the means to want is necessarily skeptics. Freedom from any kind of conviction is part of his strength, can the open eyes. The passion, the reason and the power of his being, yet enlightened and more despotic than he is to himself, - it takes all his intellect into its service (and not only in their possession), it makes safe, it gives him the courage to unholy means (even holy) begrudge them beliefs that it needs and consumes even beliefs, but it does not submit to them. That makes it only knows itself as a sovereign.

Conversely, the want of faith, for something unconditioned by yea and nay, a necessity of weakness, all weakness is weakness of will, all the weakness of the will comes from the fact that no passion, no categorical imperative commanded. The man of faith, the "believer" of any kind is necessarily a dependent type of person, i.e. one that is start not as an end, nor can ever start on its own purposes - which as a means of consumption must be... It gives an instinctive morality of selflessness is the highest honor, for their talk about it all, their wisdom, their experience, their vanity. And the belief is still a form of self-denial.

11 [49]

From the vast areas of art, which is anti-German, and will remain, and of the excluded once and for all German youths, horned Siegfried and other Wagnerian are: the genius Bizet's what a new one - oh, so old - sensitivity that so far in the educated European music had no language, to the sound, helped a southern, brown, burnt sensibility, which is certainly not to be understood by humid idealism from the north. The African fortunately, the fatalistic serenity, with an eye that looks tempting, deep and terrible, and the lascivious melancholy of the Moorish dance, the passion flashing, sharp and sudden like a dagger, and odors from the yellow afternoons of the sea approached floating in which the heart shall live for startled, as if it is to remember forgotten islands, where there once dwelt, where it would ever...

Anti-German: The buffoon. The moorish dance

The other treasures of the anti-German aesthetic enjoyment

11 [50]

The "real world", as has always been one conceives it, — it was always the apparent world once again.

11 [51]

One must have courage in the body in order to permit wickedness: most people are too cowardly to do so.

11 [52]

"Caesar among pirates"

11 [53]

and among these poets there are stallions neigh in a chaste way

11 [54]

From the reign of virtue.

How the virtue to rule helps.

A tractatus politicus.

By

Friedrich Nietzsche.

Preface.

This tractatus politicus is not for everyone's ears: it's about the politics of virtue, of their ways and means to power. That virtue seeks to rule, who would you ban it? But as them does this -! believe it or not... So this is not tractatus for everyone's ears. We have it determined that the benefit, which is keen to learn is not how virtuous, but virtuous as you make - how to bring the rule of virtue. I will even show that to want this one, the rule of virtue, the other is basically not allowed to want, just so they waived it, to be virtuous. This sacrifice is great: but perhaps such a goal is worth sacrifice. And even more!... And some of the great moralists have risk (risquirt) so much. Of these, namely already recognized the truth and anticipating what should be taught with this treatise for the first time: that the rule of virtue absolutely attainable only by the same means by which they ever attained any rule, at least not by virtue... This treatise is, as I said, in virtue of the policy: it is an ideal of this policy, he describes them as they would be if something could be perfect on this earth. Well no philosopher will be in doubt about what is the type of perfection in politics, namely the Machiavellianism. But the Machiavellianism, pure, sans melange, cru, vert, dans toute Sat force, dans toute son aprete is superhuman (ubermenschlich), divine (gottlich), transcendent, he is of people never achieving maximum striped... Even in this narrower kind of politics, politics of virtue seems to have been the ideal never attained. Even Plato has it only in passing. One discovers, supposing that you have eyes for hidden things, even the most unprejudiced and most conscious moralists (- and that's the name for such politicians of morality, for each type founders of new moral forces), traces of them, that they also of human weakness have paid their tribute. Aspirated all, to say the least in their fatigue, and for himself, for virtue: the first error and capital of a moralist, - as what the immoralist that has to be. The fact that he just cannot seem to, is another matter. Or rather, it is not one other thing: there is such a basic self-denial (in moral terms, adjustment) and into the canon of the moralist, and his very own theory of duty: without it he will never be his type get perfection. Freedom from morality, even of the truth, for the sake of that goal, which outweighs any sacrifice: the rule of morality - that is that canon. The moralists have the attitude of virtue necessary to the attitude of the truth, and their failure begins only when they of virtue give, where they lose control of the virtue, when they themselves morally, are true will. Is a great moralist, among other things, necessarily a great actor, and his danger is that its adjustment is nature unawares, as it is his ideal, his eating and his operator (operari) keep a divine way apart, everything he does, sub specie boni he must do, - his tall, distant, demanding perfect! A divine! Ideal... And is in fact mentioned that the moralist that mimics no less a model than God himself: God, the greatest immoralist fact the there who understands but remain nevertheless, what he is, the good God...

11 [55]

One should never forgive it for Christianity, which has directed such men as to base Pascal. One should never stop, just fight it in Christianity that it has the will to do to break even the strongest and noblest souls. One should never be peace as long as it is not destroyed in a land: the ideal of man, which has been invented by Christianity. The whole absurd residue of Christian fable, the term-weaving spider, and theology is not our concern, it could be a thousand times more absurd, and we would not lift a finger against him. But that ideal we fight that, with its morbid beauty and female seduction, with its secret slanderer eloquence all the cowardice and vanity cajoling weary (miidgewordener) souls - and the strongest have weary hours - such as whether all the things on in such states useful and wish most may seem, trust, innocence, modesty, patience, love for his fellows, surrender, surrender to God, a kind unharness and abdicate all his I's, is in itself the most useful and most visible (Wiinschbarste), as if the small, unassuming monster of soul, the virtuous average beast and flocks of sheep (Heerdenschaf) <type> man not only takes precedence over the stronger, more evil, covetousness, defiant, wasteful, and just about a hundred times more vulnerable species have a man, but really for the people in general, the ideal, the goal of the measure, the highest desirability. Give this establishment an ideal far the weirdest temptation to which the person was exposed to was, for him threatened the stronger more prudent exceptions and lucky accidents of man, where does the will to power and the growth of the whole type of man one step forward, the destruction, with his worthy (Werthen) should the growth of those multimen are digging at the root, which voluntarily to their higher demands and tasks sake also a more dangerous life (expressed economically: increasing business costs as much as the improbability of success) in the purchases take. What do we combat in Christianity? That it will break the strong, that it discouraged their courage, take advantage of their bad hours and fatigue, wants to run their proud assurance into anxiety and conscience (Gewissensnoth) that it knows how to make the instincts toxic and sick, until their strength, their will to turns around backwards, against himself versa, - to the strong to the excesses of self-contempt and self-abuse perish: that gruesome way of perishing, whose most famous example Pascal gives up.

11 [56]

Zola: - a certain rivalry with Taine, one of whose agents learn from them, in a skeptical milieu bring it to a kind of dictatorship. Here belongs the deliberate coarsening of the principles so that they act as a command.

11 [57]

Understand - that's sanction?

11 [58]

Themselves not to recognize: wisdom of the idealist. The idealist: a being who has reasons to stay on the dark and is smart enough to stay well above those reasons still obscure.

11 [59]

The literature of women, unsatisfied, agitated, desolate toward listening (hinhorchend) in heart and guts, with painful curiosity at any time on the imperative, from the depths of their organization categorically be formulated aut liberi aut libri: the literature of women, educated enough to understand the voice of nature even if she speaks Latin and the other ambitious enough to speak with him in secret even French: "je me verrai, je me lirai, depending m'extasierai et je dirai: possible esprit que eu tant d'j'aie?"...

The perfect woman commits literature as committing a little sin, to experiment, in passing, looking around, if anyone notices and that it observes someone: he knows how good the perfect woman is a little spot rot and brown depravity, - it knows better how everything litteratue make in woman has, as a question mark in respect to all other female modesty (Pudeur)...

11 [60]

The modern confusion.

I cannot stop what you will do with the European workers. He is much too good to now claim not to step by step more, to demand immodest: he has the least number of its own. The hope is completely over, that here is a modest and self-sufficient type of man, a less strict sense of the word slavery (Sklaventhum) in short, a state, something that has the immutability, emerging. It has made the workers' military operational: one he has the right to vote, the coalition nation (Coalitionsrecht) given: you have done everything, to the instincts, to which a worker Chinese <doer> could start to spoil: so that the worker today its existence already as a state of emergency (expressed as a morally wrong...) feels and can feel... But what you want? asked again. If you want a goal, you must want the means: if one wants slaves, - and you need them! - They do not have to educate men.

"The sum of the pain outweighs the sum of pleasure: hence the nonexistence of the world would be better than their being" like talk today is pessimism

The world is something that reasonably would not, because it causes the sentient subject is more pain than pleasure."

Pleasure and pain are minor matters, not causes; there are judgments of value, the second rank, derived first by a reigning value; a speaking in the form of feeling "useful," "harmful," and thus completely volatile and dependent. For every "useful," "harmful" are still a hundred different what? to ask.

I despise this pessimism of sensibility: he himself is a sign of deeper impoverishment of life. I will never let such a skinny ape as Hartmann of his "philosophical pessimism" is talking about. - (Ich werde nie zulassen, daB solch ein magerer Affe wie Hartmann von seinem „philosophischen Pessimismus" redet. —).

11 [62]

Talma said:

oui, nous etre sensitive Devon, Devon eprouver nous l'emotion, mais pour mieux l'imiter, pour le mieux en saisir par l'etude et la caractere reflexion. Notre art en exige de profondes. Point d'improvisation possible sur la scene, sous peine d'echec. Tout est calcul, tout doit etre prevu et l'emotion, qui semble soudain et le trouble, qui parait involontaire. - L'intonation, gesture-le, le regard qui semblent inspires, ont ete repete cent fois. Le Poet reveur cherche un beau vers, le musicien melodie une, une le geometre Demonstration: aucun d'eux d'interet n'y attache plus que nous a trouver le geste et l'accent, qui rend le mieux le sens d'un seul hemistich. Cette etude en tous lieux suit l'acteur Eprise de son art. - Faut-il vous dire plus? Nous nous sommes a nous-memes, Voyez vous quand nous notre aimons art of sujets d'observation. J'ai bien fait of pertes Cruelles; j'ai souvent resentment of chagrins Profond; he bien, apres ces premiers moments ou se fait la douleur par jour of the cris et par larmes, sentai ever un retour sur faisais qu'involontairement each measure souffrance qu'en et moi a mon insu, l'homme et l'acteur etudiait prenait sur le fait la nature. Voici de nous Devonian source fag on eprouver pour l'etre un jour emotion en etat de la rendre, mais non a l'improviste et sur la scene, quand tous les yeux sont sur nous fixes, plus rien n'exposerait notre situation. Recemment encore, depending jouais dans misanthropy Repentir et avec une actrice admirable, but jeu si si naturel pourtant reflechie et vrai et si, m'entrainait. Elle s'en apergut. Quel triomphe! pourtant et elle dit tout bas me: "Prenez garde, Talma, vous etes emu!" C'est l'effet de qu'en emotion nait le trouble; Resiste la voix, la memoire manque, sont les faux gestes, l'effet est Detruit! Ah! nous ne sommes pas la nature que nous ne sommes l'art qui ne peut tendre qu'a imiter.

Lessing sat under Moliere Destouches Minna of Minna - "un marivaudage raisonne".

11 [64]

Chinese: "as my beloved is a home (einlogirt) in my heart, I am careful to eat warm: this heat was not to be annoying"

"You yourself would see your mother die of hunger, do nothing, which is contrary to virtue."

"if you, like the tortoise, which withdraws its five limbs into its shell, your five senses pull back into yourself, so you will get it even after death in favor: you will receive the heavenly bliss"

11 [65]

"One is amazed at the number of hesitation and procrastination in the arguments of Montaigne. But on the index set in the Vatican, all parties long suspected, it is perhaps dangerous volunteered his tolerance, his maligned impartiality, the question on a kind of muted. That was a lot in his time: humanity, which questioned... "

11 [66]

Merimee superieur de vices et comme comme Joaillier chaser s difformites belongs to the movement of 1830, not by passion (she lacks -), but by the novelty of calculirten precede, and the bold choice of fabrics.

11[67]

"Bains interieurs" to express myself demurely on the nature of Madame Valmore

11 [68]

"Rien ne porte comme une bonne malheur action"

11 [69]

Sainte-Beuve: "la jeunesse est trop pour avoir du Gout Ardente.

Pour avoir du Gout, il ne suffit pas avoir d'en soi de la faculte gouter et les belles choses de l'esprit douces, il faut du loisir encore, libre et une ame vacante talk venue, comme innocente, non livery aux passions, non affairee, non bourrelee d'apres soins et d'inquietudes positive; une ame desinteressee et meme du feu exempt trop ardent de la composition, non en proie a sa propre verve insolent, il faut du repos de l'oubli, du silence, d'espace de soi near to. De que conditions, quand meme en soi on a la Faculte de trouver les, des choses pour jouir Delicate "!

11 [70]

During the performance of Christine (A. Dumas): Joanny has drawn a passport to the Queen. At the moment, to make use of that he thinks differently and closes the paper itself with the words: reservons de l'effet de plus grands besoin pour.

11 [71]

Reluctance and lust are the dumbest conceivable means of expression of judgments: which of course does not say is that the propositions which are here, according to this kind would be stupid. The omission of all reasoning and logicalness (Logicitat), or want to have a yes-no in the reduction to a passionate or pushing away, an abbreviation imperative, its usefulness is obvious: its pleasure and pain. Their origin is in the central sphere of the intellect, its condition is an infinitely accelerated perceiving, organizing, subsume, analyse, conclude: pleasure and pain are always closing phenomena, not "cause"...

The decision about what to arouse displeasure and desire is the degree of powerdependent: the same as what appears to be in terms of a small quantity of power risk and necessity of the fastest defenses may, at a greater consciousness of power, wealth a voluptuous irritation, a feeling of pleasure have as a result.

All feelings of pleasure and pain are already using for measuring overall areautility (Gesammt-Nutzlichkeit), overall area-harmfulness (Gesammt-Schadlichkeit) ahead: a sphere, where the want of a goal (state) and a selection of funds to be held. Pleasure and pain are never "original facts"

Pleasant and unpleasant emotions are volitional reactions (emotions), in which the intellect center the value of certain changes that have occurred to the fixes overall value, at the same time as the introduction of counter-actions.

11 [72]

If the world would movement a goal state, then it would be reached. The one basic fact is that they do not have goal state: and every philosophy or scientific hypothesis (i.e. the mechanism), in which such is necessary, is the one fact refuted... Seeking a world of conception (Weltconception) that this is fact do justice: the are to be explained without taking such final intentions refuge: the becoming must appeal-justified at any moment (or non-mensurable (unabwerthbar, <unvalulable>): what amounts to one), it may not be completely justified in what is present to a future or past enpresenting for the sake of contemporary. The "necessity" is not in the form of an overarching, dominant overall violence (Gesammtgewalt), or a first motor; nor less than necessary to cause something valuable. This is necessary, a overall consciousness (GesammtbewuBtsein) of becoming, to deny a "God" to the events not under the aspect of a sympathetic, confidant and nothing —meaning to bring nature: "God" is useless if he does not want something and the other is a summation of pain and lack of logic set so what would the total value of "becoming" humiliate: fortunately just missing such a sum up power (- a suffering and looking god, a "overall sensiorum (Gesammtsensorium)" and "universal spirit" - would be the greatest objection to his)

Strict: you must allow nothing at all existent - because it loses its value and becoming almost as meaningless and superfluous.

Consequently, one must ask: how has the illusion of being able to develop (have) similarly, how all value judgments, which rest on the hypothesis that there existed a being, are devalued.

But it is seen that this hypothesis of being the source of all world-libel is "the real world" "thing-in-itself (Ding an sich)" "the otherworldly world 1) becoming has no goal stated, does not lead to a "Being (Sein)".

2) becoming is no sham condition (Scheinzustand), perhaps the existent world is a appearance (Schein) 3) if the same is worth every moment: the sum of its value remains the same: in other words, it has no value, because it is missing something, what would it be measured, and in relation to which the word "value" sense would the total value of the world's non-measarable (unabwerthbar), hence the philosophical pessimism belongs among the funny things 11 [73]

The viewpoint (Gesichtspunkt) of "Werther" is the viewpoint of conservationenhancing conditions in terms of complex forms of relative life-duration within becoming:

-: there is no durable ultimate units, no atoms, no monads: here is also "being (das Seiende)" only us put into it, (for practical, useful perspective reasons) - "Sphere of control structure, (Herrschafts-Gebilde)" and the sphere of the dominant growing continuously or periodically decreasing, increasing, or, under the favor and disfavor of circumstances (the diet (Ernahrung, <nutrition>)-) - "Value" is the essential factor for the increase or decrease this stately centers ("multiplicities" in any case, but the "unity (Einheit)" is in the nature of becoming nonexistent) - a quantum of power, a becoming, so far nothing in the character of "Being (Sein)" has, so far - the means of expression of the language are useless to express the will: it is our indissoluble (unabloslichen) need of preservation, resistant a coarser world of neutral, of "things" to set and so on. Relative, we may speak of atoms and monads: and it is certain that the duration of the smallest world's most durable... there is no will: there will punctuation-which multiply resistant or lose their power

11 [74]

- that the "process of the whole" the work of humanity is not an option because there is a overall process (GesammtprozeB) (such as systems thinking (gedacht) -) gives not:

- that there is no "whole" admits that devaluation (Abwerthung) all of human existence, human goals cannot be made in regard to something that does not exist...

- that the necessity, causality, functionality useful appearances are - that non-proliferation (Vermehrung) of consciousness is the goal, but rather increase the power, in which increase the usefulness of consciousness is included, as well as with pleasure with pain - that is not the agent accepts the supreme measure of value (ie, not states of consciousness, such as pleasure and pain, if consciousness is a means of self -) - that the world is not an organism entirely, but the chaos that the development of "spirituality" is a means for relative duration of the organization is... - that all the "desirability" has no meaning in relation to the general character of Being (dafi alle „Wunschbarkeit" keinen Sinn hat in Bezug auf den Gesammtcharakter des Seins).

11 [75]

not the satisfaction of the will is the cause of lust: against this theory I will fight very superficial. The absurd psychological counterfeiting the things closest to...

but rather that the will wants to advance and again about the lord (Herr) is what stands in its way: the feeling of pleasure is precisely in the dissatisfaction of the will: the fact that he is without the limitations and obstacles still not tired enough...

11 [76]

The normal dissatisfaction of our impulses as hunger, sexual instinct, the motion drive, contains in itself absolutely nothing depressing end, it seems rather agitation (agacirend) on the lifestyle, like any rhythm of small painful stimuli, it reinforces what the pessimism prefaces us like: this dissatisfaction, rather than spoil the life is the great stimulant of life.

- One could perhaps describe the joy at all as a rhythm less pain stimuli...

11 [77]

Yes, depending on the resistors (Widerstanden), which seeks a force to about it under control, must increase the measure of the hereby challenged failure and doom (Verhangnisses): and thus any force can only omit to which resists is necessary in every action one ingredient of displeasure. Only this pain is like tear of life and strengthens the will to power!

11 [78]

The most spiritual people, provided that they are the most courageous, experience by far the most painful tragedies: but that they honor life, because it is provides them their greatest opposition.... (Die geistigsten Menschen, vorausgesetzt, daB sie die muthigsten sind, erleben auch bei weitem die schmerzhaftesten Tragodien: aber deshalb ehren sie das Leben, weil es ihnen die groBte Gegnerschaft gegenuberstellt...)

11 [79]

The means by which Julius Caesar defended himself against sickness, and headaches: tremendous marches, simple living, continuous residence in the outdoors and enduring hardship: there are, the big expected, the preservation conditions of genius at all.

11 [80]

Beware of morality: they are devalued ourselves

Caution against pity: we are overburdened with the distresses of others

Beware of "spirituality": it spoils the character by making it extremely lonely: solitude

that is untied, untied...

11 [81]

- will only be felt, but not dying (?)

11 [82]

The sense of becoming must be fulfilled at every moment, completed achieved.

11 [83]

What a good action is called, is a mere misunderstanding, and such actions are not possible.

"Egoism" is just as "selflessness" is a popular fiction, similarly, the individual, the soul.

In the vast multiplicity of events within an organism becomes conscious part of us is a mere angle: and the bit of "virtue", "selflessness" and similar fictions are punished in a completely radical way from the rest total events (Gesammtgeschehen) of lies. We do well to study our organism in its utter immorality...

The animal functions are on principle even millions of times more important than all of the beautiful states and heights of consciousness: the latter have a surplus, if they do not have to be tools for those animal functions.

The entire conscious life, together with the spirit of the soul, together with the heart, together with the quality, together with the virtue in whose service it works then?

In the greatest possible perfection of the means (food enhancers) of the basic animal functions: above all, the enhancement of life.

It is so incredibly much more to what one "body" and "meat (Fleisch)" called: the rest is a small device. The task of the whole chain of life and continues to spin (fortzuspinnen) so that the thread is more powerful - that is the task. But now may be seen, such as heart, soul, virtue, spirit conspire formally to this principal (principianti) job at run: as if they were the targets... The degeneration of life is largely due to the extraordinary ability of error (Irrthumsfahigkeit) of consciousness: it is the least by instincts in check and kept assaults therefore the longest and most thorough.

After the pleasant or unpleasant feelings that consciousness measure whether life has value: one can imagine a crazier excess of vanity? It's only one way and pleasant or unpleasant feelings are also only average! - What measures are objectively the value?

Alone in the quantity increased and power of organized, after which happens in all events, there is a will to more...

11 [84]

The "spirit" as the essence of the world recognized, as essentially the logicality (Logicitat)

11 [85]

By alcohol and hashish bring you back to levels of culture, which (at least one overcome survived) has all foods give any revelation about the past from which we were.

11 [86]

Even the way it does often enough those stupid women like that milk does not hold for food, but probably turnips (Ruben):

11[87]

All the beauty and grandeur, which we have borrowed the real and imaginary things, I will reclaim as the property and product of the man: as his fairest apology. Man as a poet, a thinker, as God, as love, as power -: oh about his royal generosity (Freigebigkeit) with which he endowed the things to be poorer and to be miserable! Previously, this was his greatest selflessness that he admired and adored, and to conceal himself knew that he was the one who has created what he admired.

11 [88]

How much unavowed (uneingestandliche) ignorant and self-satisfaction of needs is in the old religious feeling mishmash of German music backward! How much prayer, virtue, anointing, virginity, incense, and gnat (Muckerei) "closet" since talks with yet! That the music itself by words, by the term, apart from the picture: oh, how she knows them to pull up their advantage, the crafty female "eternal feminine"! even the most honest belief need not to be ashamed if that instinct is satisfied, - it remains outside. This is healthy, smart and, insofar as it expresses shame of poverty of all religious proposition, a good sign... Nevertheless, it remains a tartuffery (Tartufferie)...

If one, however, as did Wagner in his last days with dangerous falsehood, besides the religious symbolism, as in Parsifal, where he alludes to the superstitious (aberglaubischen) nonsense of the Last Supper, and not only alludes: so aroused such indignation music...

11 [89]

People have always misunderstood the love: they believe this to be unselfish, because they want the advantage of another being, often against their own advantage: they want it but that other beings have... In other cases, a finer parasitism (Schmarotzerthum) love, a dangerous and reckless nest (Sicheinnisten) a soul into another soul - sometimes in the flesh... oh! how much to "the landlord" expenses!

How much advantage does man sacrifice, like a little "selfish," he is! All his emotions and passions will have their rights - and how far from the benefits of intelligent self-interest is the affect!

You do not want to be "lucky", you must be an Englishman, to be believed, that man always seeks his own advantage, and our desires to make a mistake in a long passionate about the things - their pent-up force investigating the resistors

11 [90]

What Richard Wagner is worth, which is the first to tell us who made the best use of it. Meanwhile, you try to a value Wagner to believe, to which he himself was dying to do may think...

11 [91]

Refinement of prostitution, not abolish...

Marriage has had the longest time, the bad conscience against it: if you believe it? Yes, we believe it should.

In honor of the old women

11 [92]

I am taking the liberty to forget me. Tomorrow I will be back with me at home. (Ich nehme mir die Freiheit, mich zu vergessen. Ubermorgen will ich wieder bei mir zu Hause sein).

11 [93]

everything with which the person knows to be not yet completed, which no one has yet digested, the "mud of existence" - at least for the wisdom he remains the best fertilizer...

11 [94]

That emperor (Kaiser) was constantly before the transience of all things, so as not too important to take and remain calm between them. Everything seems to be the other way around too much value, as it should be so fleeting: I seek an eternity for any: should we pour the most precious salves and wines into the sea? - And my only consolation is that everything what was is eternal - the sea washes it out again

11 [95]

"Do you believe in the divinity of Christ": Man molested, as we know, Voltaire even in his last moments asked his Cure, and not satisfied with the fact that Voltaire, it meant that he wanted to be left alone, he repeated his question. Came over the dying man his last fury: he furiously pushed the unauthorized questioner: "au nom du dieu! - He shouted in his face - ne me parlez pas de cet homme-la immortal last words where everything is grouped together, whereas this had fought bravest spirit.

Voltaire judged: "There is nothing divine about this Jew of Nazareth": so he judged from the classic taste.

The classic taste of Christian taste and set the term "divine" in fundamentally different, and whoever has the former in the body that cannot unlike Christianity as pact (Latin: foeda, <contract>) and the Christian ideal as a caricature and vilification of the Divine (Gottlichen) received.

11 [96]

That is the culprit again in the doable into it takes, after he was pulled out of it conceptually, and thus has drained the doable; that the thing to do, "the goal", the "intention", the "purpose" in taking back the doable, after he had been artificially removed from him, and thus has drained the doable; that "all purposes", "targets", "sense" only modes of expression and metamorphoses of a will that inhere (inharirt) everything that happens, the will to power; that purpose, objectives, intentions, want ever so much as stronger-to-be want (Starker-werden-wollen) is want to grow, and it also means like;

that the most general and lowest instinct in all doable and desire for that very reason has remained unrecognized and hidden, because in practice we always follow his commandments because we are this commandment... All valuations are only consequences and stronger prospects in the service of the one will: the value estimate itself is just this will to power, a criticism of Being (Seins) out for some of these values is something absurd and misleading, even supposing that it initiates a process of destruction, this process is still in the service of this will...

Estimate Being (Sein) itself: but the estimate (Abschatzen) is of this Being (Sein) still: - and by saying no, we do still what we are... You have the absurd (Absurditat) view that existence (daseinsrichtenden) directing gesture, and look then to guess yet, what is actually thus betakes. It is symptomatic.

11[97]

The philosophical nihilist is convinced that all that happens is meaningless and unfair (umsonstig) and there should be no senseless and unfair (umsonstiges) Being (Sein). But where did this: it should not? But how do you take this "sense"? this measure? - The nihilist says basically, the terms of such a useless bleak Being (Sein) acts upon a philosopher unsatisfactory, desolate, desperate, and such insight goes against our finer sensibility as philosophers. It amounts to the absurd well value (Werthung): the character of existence (Daseins) the philosopher would be a pleasure, if indeed it is right to exist...

Now it is easy to understand, that have pleasure and displeasure in the event only the sense of means can be: it would ask remains, whether we call the "sense" and "purpose" look at all could, if not the question of meaninglessness (Sinnlosigkeit) or its opposite for us is unsolvable.

11 [98]

Value of transience (Verganglichkeit): something that has no duration, which contradicts itself, has little value. But the things to which we believe as permanent, as such, are pure fiction. If everything flows, it is a quality of transience (Verganglichkeit) (the "truth") and the duration and immortality just an illusion (Schein).

11 [99]

Critique of Nihilism.

1.

The Nihilism as psychological state will have to come first if we have a "sense" have searched in all events, is not there: so that the seeker finally loses courage. Nihilism is because the recognition of the long waste of strength, the agony of the "vain," insecurity, lack of opportunity to recover somehow, somewhere over to calm down yet the shame from themselves, as they had too long cheated... That meaning was could be: the "fulfillment" of a moral highest canon in all events, the moral world order, or the growth of love and harmony in the intercourse of beings; or approaching a state of universal happiness, or even that assail a general nothing state (Nichts-Zustand) - is a goal still a sense. The common element in all these modes of representation that a something through the process itself is achieved will be: - and then one realizes that becoming nothing achieved, nothing will be achieved... So the disappointment over an alleged aim of becoming the cause of nihilism: whether it in terms of a very specific purpose, whether it generalizes the insight into the inadequacy of all previous endhypotheses (Zweck-Hypothesen) relating to the whole "evolution" (- the man no longer staffs (Mitarbeiter), much of the focus of them).

Nihilism as a psychological state enters the second one, if you have a wholeness, a systematization (Systematisirung), itself one organizing has all happened and recognized among all happened: so that in the total concept of a supreme governance and administration form revels for admiration and reverence thirsty soul (- it is the soul of a logician, it already meets the absolute logic and dialectic, to reconcile all things...) A kind of unity, some form of "monism" and in consequence of this belief of man in deep relationship and dependency feeling of a whole infinitely superior to him, a mode of divinity... "The good of the universal demands the devotion of the individual"... but lo (aber siehe da) and behold, it gives no such universal! Basically, man has lost faith in its value if it does not act through an infinitely valuable whole: he conceives that such a whole has, to believe in its value can.

Nihilism as a psychological state has yet a third and final form. These two insights given that will which nothing is to be achieved and that underneath all becoming there is no grand unity in which the allowed individuals to submerge completely, as the highest in an element values: there remains as an excuse left, than this whole world of becoming to condemn deception and to invent a world that lies beyond it, as the real world. But as soon discovers the man is fashioned as only for psychological needs of this world and how he completely and has no right, we obtain the last form of nihilism, which the lack of faith in a metaphysical world within itself, - which is the belief to a real world forbids. At this point gives you the reality of becoming as one with reality, forbids oneself every kind of secret routes to rear and false divinities - but not endure this world that wants to deny you have not...

- What happened in fact? The feeling of worthlessness (Werthlosigkeit) was achieved, as it was understood that neither the term "purpose", with the term "unity", with the term "truth" is the general character of existence may interpreted (interpretirt).

Nothing is achieved and thus reached, it lacks the overarching unity in the multiplicity of events: the character of existence (Daseins) is not "true", is wrong (falsch)... you have absolutely no reason to persuade themself a true world...

In short (Kurz): the categories of "purpose (Zweck)", "unity (Einheit)", "Being (Sein)" with whom we have a value placed in the world are, again we pulled out - and now sees the world from valuesless <worthless> (nun sieht die Welt werthlos aus)...

2.

Suppose that we have realized how far into these three categories, the world is not designed and may be that after this recognition, the world begins to be worthless for us: we must ask, where is our faith in these three categories - we try to if it is not possible, they terminate to the faith. We have these three categories depreciates, then the proof of their inapplicability to the universe no longer a reason to all the depreciation.

* *

Result: the belief in the categories of reason is the cause of nihilism - we have measured the value of the world according to categories, which refer to a purely fictitious world. (Resultat: der Glaube an die Vernunft-Kategorien ist die Ursache des Nihilismus, — wir haben den Werth der Welt an Kategorien gemessen, welche sich auf eine rein fingirte Welt beziehen)

* *

Final result (SchluB-Resultat): all the values, with which we have searched far the world's first of us to make valuable and finally give it depreciates have, as they proved unequipped (unanlegbar) - all these values are, psychologically, the results of certain perspectives of utility to maintain and increasing human domination structure: and only falsely projected into the nature of things. It is still the hyperbolic naivete of man himself as a measure of value and meaning of things... (SchluB-Resultat: alle Werthe, mit denen wir bis jetzt die Welt zuerst uns schatzbar zu machen gesucht haben und endlich ebendamit entwerthethaben, als sie sich als unanlegbar erwiesen — alle diese Werthe sind, psychologisch nachgerechnet, Resultate bestimmter Perspektiven der Niitzlichkeit zur Aufrechterhaltung und Steigerung menschlicher Herrschafts-Gebilde: und nur falschlich projicirt in das Wesen der Dinge. Es ist immer noch diehyperbolische Naivetat des Menschen, sich selbst als Sinn und WerthmaB der Dinge...)

11 [100]

The highest values, life in the service of man should, in particular their disposal when they are very difficult and costly over him: these social values you have for the purpose of sound reinforcement, such as would be if they commands God, as "reality" as "real" world, as hope and future world built on the people. Now that the shabby origin of these values is clear, the all seems so devalued, "pointless (sinnlos, <meaningless>)"... but that's just become one intermediate state (aber das ist nur ein Zwischenzustand).

11 [101]

I certainly do not wish to play at the contemptible comedy, which still today, especially in Prussia, philosophical pessimism is called; I see even the necessity not to speak of them. With disgust, you should have long ago turned away from the spectacle of that skinny ape which Mr. Hartmann gives: in my view is that any line through that he had referred the names with the same time Schopenhauer in his mouth.

11 [102]

That one's own acts committed against cowardice. That they were not behind him in the lurch... The bite of conscience is indecent.

11 [103]

That is the last human values back into the comer nicely put back where they have only one right: as loafer-values. There are many kinds of animals have disappeared, even supposing that the man would disappear, so nothing would be lacking in the world. You must be philosopher enough to even this to admire nothing (- to be surprised by nothing cLatin: Nile admirari> -)

11 [104]

Is it about the "why?" Of his life in harmony with yourself, then gives you the how? cheaply. It is itself a sign of disbelief in why, and sense of purpose, a lack of will, if the value of pleasure and pain comes to the fore and find lessons hearing hedonistic pessimism, and self-denial, resignation, virtue, "objectivity " may already be the slightest sign that it begins to lack the main thing.

That you know to give yourself a goal (Ziel)

11[105]

NB. a mob-man, a rancor-man, a buttercup (Rankunkel)...

11 [106]

Not to be confused: - The disbelief as inability ever to believe and, on the other hand, as a failure something more to believe: in the latter case commonly a symptom of a new faith (Glauben)

Unbelief (Unglauben) as is the inability to negate disability — he knows that he is neither a yes nor to defend against a no...

11 [107]

Idleness is the beginning of all philosophy. - Therefore - philosophy is a vice...? (MuBiggang ist aller Philosophic Anfang. — Folglich — ist Philosophie ein Laster?...)

11 [108]

A philosopher recovers differently and in others: he is recovering as example in nihilism. The belief that there is no truth, the nihilist-faith is a big one for stretching limbs, the ceaselessly as a warrior of knowledge is a loud ugly truths in the struggle. Because the truth is ugly

11 [109]

If one settles with the music, the dramatic music: good music is still enough left

11 [110]

We also believe in the virtue but the virtue in the Renaissance style, virtu, virtue moraline.

11 [111]

How is it that the fundamental article of faith in psychology together with all (allesammt) the worst distortions and counterfeiting (Falschmunzereien) are wrong? "Man strives for happiness" for example - what's so true! In order to understand what life is, what kind of struts and stress is life, must apply the formula as well as plant and tree of the beast. "What are striving to plant?" - But here we have already forged a false unity that there is not: the "fact of a million-fold growth with their own and half own initiatives is hidden and denied, if we have a crude unit" to suppress "plant" (Pflanze). " That the last smallest "individuals" is not understandable in the sense of a "metaphysical individual" and atom, that their sphere of influence constantly shifts - that is first visible but seeks a Each of them when it is transformed in such a way to "happiness"? - But all the self-spreading, incorporation, growth is one aiming to counter, movable is essential to do with pain states allied (Verbundenes): it has, what drives here, at least something different to when it wants in such a way the pain and seeks constantly. - What the trees of a jungle fight with each other? Get "lucky"? - In order to power...

The man who became master of the forces of nature, master of his own wildness and lawlessness: follow the desires have, have learned to be useful.

The man, compared to a pre-humans (Vor-Menschen), represents a tremendous quantity of power is - not a plus of "happiness": how can one say that after happiness sought is...?

11 [112]

The higher man is different from the low in terms of the fearlessness and the challenge of the accident: it is a sign of decline when they start hedonistic measure of value to be regarded as the top (- physiological fatigue, willpower depletion -) Christianity, with its perspective on "salvation" is a typical mindset for a suffering and impoverished human species: to create a full power will suffer, suffer go: it is the Christian bigots healing a bad music and hieratic gestures one annoyance

11 [113]

Toward the psychology and epistemology (Erkenntnisslehre).

I think the phenomenality and the inner set world: everything, what we realize is trimmed through and through until simplified schematized (schematisirt) designed - the actual process of inner "perception" that causal association (Causalvereinigung) between thoughts, feelings, desires, such as the between subject and object, completely hidden from us - and perhaps a pure imagination. This "apparent internal world is treated with exactly the same forms and procedures, such as the "outer" world. We never come to "facts": pleasure and pain are late and intellect-derived phenomena...

The "causality" escapes us; be assumed between thought a direct causal band, as does the logic - that is a consequence of the crudest and clumsiest observation between playing two thoughts nor all the possible affects their play: but the movements are too fast, so ignore we do, deny it, we...

"Thinking" as the start is epistemological, not before: that is a completely arbitrary fiction, achieved by singling out one element from the process and subtracting all the rest, for the purpose of an artificial grooming understanding of publication (V erstandlichung)...

The "spirit", something that is thinking: maybe even "the spirit absolute, pure, pure (rein, pur)" - this conception is a derived second consequence of the false introspection which believes in "thinking" is only an act imagination (imaginirt) that does not occurs, "thinking" and secondly, a subject-imaginirt substrate in which each act of this thinking and nothing else has its origin: that is, both the doable (Thun), as are the doer fictitious

11 [114]

"want (Wollen <wish>)" is not "desirable", aiming to ask: of which it stands out by the emotion of the command's

there is no "want", but rather only one thing-want: you do not have the target trigger from the state: as do the epistemological (ErkenntniBtheoretiker). "Shall" as they understand it comes from as little as "thinking" is a pure fiction.

that something is commanded, belongs to the will (:this is not to say that the will "effected (effektuirt)" is...)

That general stress state in virtue of which a force may seek release - is not a

"want"

11 [115]

In a world that is significantly wrong, truth would be an unnatural tendency: such could only sense than a means to a specific higher power of falsehood: so that a world of truth, being able to be fictitious, first had the true riches to be made (counting that such is "truly" believe)

Simple, transparent, with no conflict, permanently, is consistent, without wrinkle, sleight, curtain, form: the way a person conceives a world of Being (Seins) as "God" after his image (nach seinem Bilde).

Thus truth is possible, the whole sphere of man to be very clean, small and respectable: it has the advantage to be in every sense on the part of the conscientious. Lies, deceit, dissembling, must excite astonishment...

The hatred of the lie and the adjustment of pride, of an irritable sense of honor, but there is also such a hatred of cowardice because lying is prohibited. - For a different "Thou shalt not lie" kind of person helps everything moralizing nothing against the instinct, which requires proof of the lie: the testimony of New Testament.

11 [116]

There are those who seek it, where something is immoral, if they judge "this is wrong", they believe that we should abolish it and change. Conversely, I did not rest as long as I am with a matter (Sache) not yet aware of their immorality. I have this out, so my balance is restored.

11[117]

An exuberant spirit of the dance is the natural movement of every reality and loves to touch it with his toes, is hateful to indulge in sad things

11[118]

we Hyperboreans

My conclusion is: that the real man has a much higher value represents as the "desirable" man of any previous ideal, that all the "desirability" were in regard to man absurd and dangerous excesses, with a single type of man their conservation and wants to hang growth conditions on the human race as a law, that each to power brought "desirability" such origin until now the value of man, his strength, his future certainty depressed is, that the wretchedness and angle of intellectualism (Winkel-Intellektualitat) of the people at most merely represents, even today, if he wishes, that the ability of people to set values, previously developed was too low to the actual, not merely "desirable" values of the people to justice, that the ideal world until now, the fact - and slandering human power (menschverleumdende), the poisonous breath of reality, the great seduction (Verfuhrung) to nothingness was...

11 [119]

To preface.

I describe what is coming: the advent of nihilism. I can describe here, because here some needful betakes itself - the signs of it are everywhere, the eyes are missing for this character yet. I praise, I blame not, that it comes: I think there is one of the greatest crises, a moment of deepest self-reflection (Selbstbesinnung des Menschen) of human beings: whether humans are of them recovered, though he is master of this crisis, this is a question of its force: it is possible...

The modem man thinks a trial basis soon to this, now at those value and drops him then: the circle of survived and dropped value is always full, and the emptiness (Leere) and poverty of rated (Werthen) is always more to the feeling, the movement is unstoppable - although in large style of the delay is trying

Finally he ventured a critique of the values at all, he recognizes its source, he recognizes enough to believe in no value, the pathos is there, the new thrill (Schauder)...

What I relate is the history of the next two centuries...

11 [120]

That adequate between subject and object a kind of relationship takes place, that the object is something of interior saw would be subject, is a good-natured invention, which, I think, has had its day. The measure of what we at all aware, is so utterly dependent on gross utility of becoming conscious of how we allowed this kind of consciousness angle perspective (Winkelperspektive) on a "subject" and "object" statements, which would affect the reality!

11 [121]

one can be the lowest and most primitive activity in the protoplasm does not derive from a desire for self-preservation, for it takes a nonsensical way more to himself than require the preservation of dignity and, above all, it "shall be" so just do not, but decays... The drive that works here, has just this self-not-get-willing (Sich-nicht-erhaltenWollen) to declare: "hunger" is already an interpretation, not equal to more complex organisms (- Hunger is a specialization (spezialisirte) and later form of the instinct, an expression of labor (Arbeitstheilung), about the service of a higher ruling instinct)

11 [122]

- this is not what we deposited: that we find no God, neither in history nor in nature, or behind nature - but rather (sondem) that we do what was worshiped as a God, not as "divine (gottlich)", but rather (sondern) as holy visage (Fratze), as effervesce (Moutonnerie), as absurd and pitiable silliness (Niaiserie), as the principle of world and man defamation (Mensch-Verleumdung) feel: in short, that we deny God as God. It is the height of psychological mendacity of man, a being as the beginning and "in-itself" a new position his angular scale of it is just good, wise, powerful, valuable calculate out the phenomenal - and the whole causality, in virtue of which any any goodness, any wisdom, any power exists and has value indispensable. In short, elements of the latest and caused most of origin deemed to be incurred, but to set a "per se" and perhaps even as a cause of all incurred at all... Let's get out of the experience of any case where a person is significantly above the measure of human collected has, we see that every high degree of power, freedom of good and evil as well as of "true" or "wrong" in itself does and what quality will may treat any bill, we understand the same again for each high degree of wisdom - the goodness in it as well as lifted the truthfulness, justice, virtue, and other folk leanings of valuing. Finally, any high degree of goodness itself: it is not apparent that he already presupposes an intellectual myopia and inelegance? Similarly, the inability to distinguish between true and false distinction between useful and harmful to a greater distance to go? Not to mention that bring a high degree of power in the hands of the highest quality, the most disastrous consequences ("the abolition of evil") would give rise to? - In fact, you only see at what inspires the "god of love," his faithful for trends: they ruin humanity in favor of the "good" - in practice, has the same God in view of the real nature of the world as God the highest myopia, devilry (Teufelei, <evil trick>) and impotence proved: from which there results, how much value its conception.

That alone is knowledge and wisdom has no value, any more than kindness: you must always have the goal yet, from where will these properties worth or worthlessness it could be a target, from which represented an extreme knowledge of a high unworthy (Unwerth, <unvalued>) (e.g. where the extreme deception would be one of the requirements of the increase of life, similarly, if paralyze the goodness around the springs of the great desire and discourage would be able...

Our human life is given, as it is, all "truth" has all the "goodness" all "holiness," all "divinity" in the Christian style far proved to be a major threat - yet now mankind is in danger of a adverse life-ideality to perish

11[123]

The advent (Heraufkunft) of nihilism.

Nihilism is not the only one contemplativeness about that, and not only the belief that everything is worthy to perish "in vain": you put in hand, we aimed to basically... That is, if you will, illogical: but the nihilist does not believe in the nescessity to be logical... It is the condition of strong spirits and wills: and such it is not possible to stay with the 'no' to stand 'of the sentence the no indeed comes from their nature. The destruction (Ver-Nichtung) by the sentence seconded the destruction (Ver-Nichtung) by the hands.

11 [124]

If we are "disappointed", so we are not there in terms of life: but that we have risen above the "desirability" of any kind eyes. We view with a scornful indignation at the what "ideal" means that we despise us just about every hour to keep down not that absurd impulse to what is called "idealism". The pampering is stronger than the wrath of disappointed...

11 [125]

The immaturity of the perfect moralist, and what our hidden self many skinned (vielhautigen) pretensions, just to be, who say "give you, as you are" as if it would not only be something that is...

11 [126]

IV NB. The selection of equals, the "exodus", the isolation

11[127]

NB. against justice... At J. Stuart Mill: I for see horror (perhorreszire) his meanness, which says "what is the right one, the others are cheap, what you do not want, etc., which also add to any one else", which the whole human traffic reciprocity of power seeks to explain so that each action appears as a kind of redemption for something that is proven to us. Here is the prerequisite undistinguished in the lowest sense: here is the equivalence of the values of actions provided for me and you, here is the most personal value of an action simply annulled (that which can be compensated by anything and paid for -) The "reciprocity" is a great meanness, just that something that I do, not be done by someone else would and could, that no compensation should be - except in the most select sphere of "my equal," inter pares that in a deeper sense never gives back, because something is unique and only does unique - this basic conviction contains the cause of aristocratic separation from the crowd, because the amount of "equality" and therefore compensable, and "reciprocity" believes.

11 [128]

It is the feeling of kinship, which connects the children of a nation: this relationship is physiologically a thousand times stronger than commonly assumed. Language, customs, common interests and fates - that is all that much to understand oneself, to the same due to ancestors.

11 [129]

the decline of the German spirit, which has grown with the advent of father land (Vaterlanderei) nationalism and the step

11 [130]

No one talks to the woman of veracity: "Give yourself the way you are" means to wife talked almost the opposite of what it means as a call to the man

11 [131]

— not for his faith, he is burned, with little green wood: but for the fact that he has no courage to his faith more.

11 [132]

— a man, like his, he should: the sounds to us as absurd as "a tree, as it should be"

11[133]

NB. One recognizes the superiority of the Greek people, the Renaissance man but you would have without him its causes and conditions: the Greeks to this day lack a deeper insight

11 [134]

"Things that have a quality in itself" - a dogmatic idea with which we must absolutely break

11 [135]

For a critique of big words. -1 am full of suspicion and malice against what is called "ideal": here is my pessimism to have recognized as the "higher feelings" that are a source of disaster reduction and the lowering of the value of people.

- one is deceived every time you have a "progress" expected from an ideal: the ideal of victory every time so far was a retrograde movement.

- Christianity, revolution, the abolition of slavery, equal rights, philanthropy, love of peace, justice, truth: all these big words have value only in stuggle (Kampf), as standard: not as realities but rather as a ceremonial words (Prunkworte) for something completely different (even opposite!)

11 [136]

Criticism of big words. "Freedom" for the determination of power "Justice"

"Equality of Rights"

"Brotherhood"

"Truth" (in sects, etc.

11[137]

The "growing autonomy of the individual" shall talk of this Parisian philosophers, such as Fouillee: they should only look at the race moutonniere that they themselves are...!

Power but the eye on, their future masters sociologist!

The "individual" has become strong under reverse conditions: it describes the extreme weakness and atrophy of the people, they want their own needs and to the entire apparatus of the old ideal of lies! you are the type, that you present your herd really needs-as ideal feels!

The complete lack of psychological honesty!

11 [138]

The origin of the ideal, examination of the soil on which it grows.

A. Proceed from the "aesthetic" states, where the world is full of round, saw a perfect will-the pagan ideal: self-affirmation is the dominant of the buffon

the highest type: the classical ideal - as an expression of prosperity has turned out one of the main instincts

- is again the highest style: style of the great expressions of the "will to power" itself (the most feared instinct dares to confess)

- it gives off

B. Proceed from states where the world is empty, paler, diluted seen is where the "spirituality" and sensuousness takes the rank of perfection, is avoided where the most brutal, brutish direct (Thierisch Direkte), next: the "manner", "the angel "(priestly = virgin (jungfraulich) = ignorant) physiological characteristics of such" idealists "...

the anemic ideal: under certain circumstances it may be the ideal of such natures, which the first, the pagan pose (:as in Spinoza, Goethe sees his "holy")

- from one expects, you choose

C. Proceed from states where we experience the world of absurd, poor, poorer, more deceptive, as we suspect that in their ideal or even want: the projection of the ideal in the natural resistance, resistance, actual, logical contradiction. The condition of that the so judges (- the "impoverishment" of the world as a result of suffering: it takes, not gives you more -)

: the unnatural ideal - be negated, it destroyed

(The Christian ideal is an intermediate form between the second and third, mostly with this soon, now with that shape.)

the three ideals of life

A. Either an amplification (pagan)

B. or a dilution

(anemic)

C. or a denial

(unnatural)

the "deification" felt in the highest abundance in selection of the most delicate in the destruction and disregard for life.

<Translator: for the above formating check the German>

11 [139]

The level of tension, resistance, the risk of legitimate distrust, the degree to be brought into the victims of human life in which the probability of failure is high, yet the ventures is risky:

11 [140]

The herd-ideals (Heerdenthier-Ideale) - now culminating as the highest value heading of "society" attempt to give it a cosmic, yes metaphysical value (ihr einen kosmischen, ja metaphysischen Werth zu geben)

I am defending them against the Aristotelianism.

A society, which in itself that consideration and delicacy preserved in terms of freedom, must feel as an exception and to have a power against which they stand out, against whom it is hostile and looks down

- the more I make right and put me right, the more I get (gerathe) under the rule of average, and finally the most numerous

- the requirement (Voraussetzung, < presupposition>) that an aristocratic society has in him, to get between its members with high degrees of freedom, the extreme tension, which in the presence of the opposite impulse originates in all members: the will to power...

11 [141]

if you want to remove the strong contrasts and diversity rank, so it creates the strong love that high-mindedness, the sense of being-in-itself off too.

11 [142]

For the real psychology of freedom and equality society:

what decreases? The will to self-responsibility - sign of the decline of autonomy the military and weapons capability (Waffentiichtigkeit) to command the force - even in the most spiritual the sense of awe, of subordination, of silence-rounder, the passion, the great task of the tragedy, the hilarity (Heiterkeit)

11 [143]

Chapter:

Criticism of big words. From the origin of the ideal.

the herd-ideal

How to bring virtue to rule. The circle of philosophers, the ascetic ideal

The religious ideal.

Physiology of the ideal I. II III.

the men's ideal

The political ideal.

"Science"

the ideal of spirituality

III the herd-ideal

III the men's ideal

I the ideal of anti-nature

II the ideal of spirituality

I the pagan ideal

III the hermit ideal (Stoa, etc.)

II the ideal of sensualisation

Panel:

From the origin (Herkunft) of the ideal

A. the herd-ideal

their ideal of the gentleman their ideal of the hermit

B. the pagan ideal

the ideal of anti-nature

C. the ideal of sensualisation the ideal of spiritualization

the ideal of the dominant emotion

Criticism of big words.

Truth.

Justice.

Love you.

Peace.

Virtue

Freedom.

Goodness

Righteousness

Genius

Wisdom

11 [144]

Pascal: le pire est celui times, qu'on fait par bonne intention. < is the worst times, we do by good intentions>

11 [145]

Role of "consciousness"

It is essential that you look at the role of "consciousness" does not lay hands: our relationship with the "outside world", which it has developed. In contrast, the directorate, respectively, the care and forethought in terms of the interplay of bodily functions, we shall not in consciousness, any more than the spiritual a magazine loading (Einmagazinirung): that it gives a supreme authority, must not be doubted: a kind of guiding committee, where the various main desires their voice and assert power. "Lust", "pain" are hints from this sphere: the... will act similarly,. The ideas similarly,

In summa: what is conscious, is under causal relationships that are withheld from us altogether, - the succession of thoughts, feelings, ideas in the mind expresses nothing about it, that this sequence is a causal consequence: it is apparently so in the highest degree. This plausibility out we have our whole conception of spirit, reason, logic, etc. established (that there is not all: they are fictitious and syntheses units)... And this again in the things behind the projected things!

Usually, one takes consciousness itself as a body-sensorium and supreme authority: however, there is only one means of communicability (Mittheilbarkeit): it is developed in traffic and in terms of transport interests... "Traffic" here understood by the influences of the outside world and the necessary reactions on our part here; just as well as our reactions to the outside. It is not the line, but rather an organ of the line

11 [146]

The means by virtue of which a stronger species maintains itself.

To concede a right to exceptional acts, as an attempt at self-control and freedom Go into states where it is not allowed, not to be barbarian

Obtain any kind of asceticism by a superior force and certainty in terms of his will power. Not to communicate, the silence, beware of the charm.

Learn to obey, in the sense that it gives off a sample for self-maintenance. Casuistry of honor point driven into the finest (Casuistik des Ehrenpunktes ins Leinste getrieben). Never close, "which one is right, the others are cheap" - but vice versa!

The retaliation, the return - may (Zuriickgeben-durfen) be treated as a privilege to concede a distinction

The virtue of others not ambition (ambitioniren).

11 [147]

Theory of sex drive: "the 'homunculi', which unite desire into existence, their desire to live in one-collective desire, the consciousness that observes and for his own need of taking " - Renan's words Hartley Louillee p 217.

11 [148]

The time comes when we are sure to must pay for two thousand years Christians to have been long: we lose the focus, let the live us - we have a long time know not where, yet one. We plunge headlong into the opposite value evaulation, with an equal volume of energy with which we have been Christians - with the absurd exaggeration of the Christian, we

1) the "immortal soul", the eternal value of the "person"

2) the solution, the direction, the well value in "beyond"

3) the moral value as the highest value, the "salvation of the soul," as cardinalinterest

4) "Sin," "ground," "flesh," "desire" - as "the world" stigmatizes.

Now everything is false through and through, "word", confused, weak or spans

a) attempting a kind of earthly solution, but in the same sense in which the ultimate triumph of truth, love, justice of socialism: "equality of persons"

b) one also tried the moral ideal to hold (with the primacy of unegoistic, selfdenial, the negation of will)

c) one even tried to hold the "beyond": if only, as an anti-logic x: but you have clothes immediately so that a kind of metaphysical solace in the old style can be drawn from it

d) one trying to divine guidance in the old style, the rewarding, punishing, educating, for the better order of things, leading from the event pick out

e) one still believes in good and evil: so that the victory of good and evil as the destruction of the task feels (- that is English, a typical case of flathead John Stuart Mill)

f) the scorn of the "naturalness" of desire, the ego: attempt even the highest spirituality and art as a result of depersonalization and disinterestedness as to understand

g) one allows the church, still intrude into all important experiences and main points of the individual life, to give them consecration, higher meaning to be: we also have a "Christian state", the Christian "marriage"

11 [149]

The perfect nihilism

its symptoms: the great contempt

the great compassion the great destruction

its culmination point (Culminations-Punkt): a doctrine which even the life, disgust, pity and the desire to destroy excites, as absolutely and eternally teaches

11 [150]

The history of European nihilism.

The period of uncertainty, the tentative nature of all to preserve (conserviren) the old and the new drive cannot.

The period of clarity: you realize that the old and the new basic differences are: the old values from declining, the new one from the rising life bom knowledge of nature and history are no more such "hopes" allowed - that all the old ideals are ideals hostile (born out of the decadence and the decadence determine how well the magnificent wall of morality Sunday) - we understand the old are not long and strong enough for a new one.

The period of three great passions of contempt of compassion the destruction

The period of disaster (Katastrophe)

the emergence of a doctrine which people sifting... which drives the weak to make decisions and also the strong

11 [151]

Insight that the "free spirits" is missing: the same discipline, which enables a strong nature to be strengthened and great enterprises, broken and stunted the mediocre. : the doubt

: la largeur <de coeur>

: the experiment :the independence.

11 [152] my "future"

a tough formation <education> Polytechnic (eine stramme Polytechniker-Bildung) Military service (Militardienst): so that, on average, every man is an officer of the higher classes, he was usually what he was

11 [153]

The vicious and unbridled: their depressing effect on the value of desires. It is the horrible barbarity of manners, which, especially in the Middle Ages, forcing a veritable "League of Virtue" - along with equally gruesome excesses of what the value of the human mind. The fighting "civilization" (taming) needs every kind of iron and torture to maintain itself against terribleness and beast of prey, nature upright.

This confusion is quite natural, although the worst effect: what people in power and the will to ask themselves, also gives a measure for what they are allowed to admit to himself. Would be transferred even though they may do things in respect of which a lesser man of vice and intemperance: such natures are the opposite of the vicious and unbridled.

Here the concept of harm "equivalency of the people before God (Gleichwerthigkeit der Menschen vor Gott)" extraordinary: one forbade actions and attitudes, which include, in itself, to the prerogatives of the strongly constituted (Starkgerathenen) advisable - as if they were unworthy of the human. They brought the whole tendency of people strong into disrepute, by setting up the defenses of the most vulnerable (including to the most vulnerable) as the value standard (Werth-Norm).

The confusion goes so far that you really the great virtuosos of the branded life (whose autonomy the sharpest contrast to the vicious and "unbridled" gives up) with the ignominious name. Even now believed to have disapproved of a Cesare Borgia: it's easy to laugh. The church has done on account of their vices German Emperor in thrall, as if a monk or priest should have a say about what a Friedrich the Second should ask themselves. A Don Juan is sent to hell: that is very naive. Did you notice the absence in heaven all the interesting people?... Just a hint for the female, where they find their salvation at best... Think you a little bit consistently and also with a deeper insight into what is a "great man" there can be no doubt that the church all the "great men" sent to hell - it fights (kampft) against all "greatness of man"...

11 [154]

The "honor-concept": based on a belief in "good society", in knightly main qualities of the obligation to represent themselves constantly. Much: that his life is not important to take; that one necessarily on most respectful manners, holds the part of all with whom it touches (to say the least, as far as not to "us" part) that neither confidential nor good-natured, yet funny, yet modest, except among equals, that they are always represented...

11 [155]

New Testament

The war against the noble and powerful, as it is conducted in the New Testament, is a war like that of the Reineke and with the same means: only in priestly anointing always and resolutely refusing (Ablehnung), to do his own cleverness (Schlauheit).

11 [156]

One speaks of the "profound injustice" of the social pact: as if the fact that this under favorable, those bom under adverse conditions, an injustice was, or even that it is bom with these properties, those with those... This is essential to fight. The false concept of "individual" leads to this nonsense. The circumstances in which a person grows to isolate him and him as a "spiritual monad", as it merely into dropping or set: is a consequence of the wretched souls of metaphysics (ist eine Folge der elenden SeelenMetaphysik). No one has properties it may, neither God nor his parents, no one is responsible, that he is that he is so and so that it is under these circumstances... The thread of life, he is now is not disentangled from all what was and must be: because it is not the result of a long goal is none at all will be an "ideal human" or "ideal is of happiness" or "ideal of morality," it is absurd to go somewhere "pass" want: as if somewhere would be a responsibility (Verantwortung).

The revolt of the "suffering" against

God Society Nature Drive up Education, etc.

imagine responsibilities and forms of will, it does not exist. One should not be a wrong to talk in cases where no pre-conditions for right and wrong are there. That one soul every soul in itself is the same - or equal should be: this is the worst kind of optimistic enthusiasm (optimistischer Schwarmerei). The reverse is what is desirable, the greatest possible contrast (Unahnlichkeit) and hence friction, struggle (Kampf), contradiction, and, what is desirable is the real, fortunately!

11 [157]

The intent of equal rights, and finally on the same needs, an almost inevitable consequence of our kind civilization of trade and political voice equivalency brings the exclusion and the slow extinction of the higher, more dangerous, bizarre and summa newer people with him: the experimentation to speak, hear, and a certain stop is achieved.

11 [158]

The revolt-pessimism (instead of "indignation-pessimism")

11 [159]

For "great disgust": partly because suffering, partly

self generating

the nervous-Catholic-erotic literature

the literature-pessimism France I Flaubert. Zola. Goncourt. Baudelaire,

the chez Magny dinners

For "big pity"

Tolstoy, Dostoyevsky Parsifal

11 [160]

The true civilization is, after Baudelaire, dans la diminution du Peche originel. B

11 [161]

Le Frangais est un animal de basse-cour domestique si bien, qu'il n'ose Franchir aucune stockade. B

C'est un animal de race gelatin: ne lui l'ordure deplait pas dans son domicile, et, en litterature, il est scatophage. II raffole of excrements... B

11 [162]

Tartuffe. Not a comedy, but a pamphlet. An atheist, if he happens to be a man of good education is, is, in terms of the play, think, some serious questions that we shall never surrender the rabble. B ctranslator Baudelaire>

11 [163]

Baudelaire speaks in terms of Petronius terrifiantes impuretes ses, ses buffoonery attristantes

Nonsense: but symptomatic...

11 [164]

genus irritable vatum

11 [165]

as Trimalchion who wipes his hands on the hair of his slave...

11 [166]

vecus livres, poemes vecus.

11 [167]

Byron: talkative. Mais, en revanche, ces sublime Default, qui font le grand Poet: diabolique la melancholy inseparable toujours du sentiment du beau et une personnalite Ardente, un esprit salamandra.

11 [168]

"... Il n'ya parmi les hommes de grand que le Poet, le Pretre et le soldat: l'homme qui chante, l'homme qui Benite, l'homme qui se sacrifie et sacrifie. Le reste n'est que pour le fait fouet..."

11 [169]

"Il n'ya de gouvernement raisonnable et que l'assure aristocratique. Ou republique monarchy, base sur la democratic, et sont egalement faibles absurd. "

11 [170]

"Avant tout etre un grand homme et un pour soi meme saint."

11 [171]

"Dieu est le seul etre qui, pour rain, n'a meme pas besoin d'exister."

11 [172]

On the theory of "devotion"...

L'amour, c'est le gout de la prostitution. Il n'est meme pas de plaisir noble, qui ne puisse etre a la ramene prostitution. L'etre le plus prostitution, c'est l'etre par excellence, c'est

Dieu. Dans un spectacle, dans un bal jouit chacun de tous. Qu'est-ce que l'art? Prostitution

L'amour d'un peut derive sentiment Genereux: Le Gout de la prostitution. Mais il est bientot corrompu par le gout de la Propriete.

11 [173]

Femineite de l'Eglise de la raison de son omnipuissance commenters.

11 [174]

That love is like the ordeal or a surgical operation. One is that both of the executioner or the surgeon ever.

What is the greatest pleasure of love? Has been asked in the presence of Baudelaire's. One replied, in receiving, the other one: give yourself-in. He said: lust of pride, that: lust of humility (volupte d'humilite) All these foulmouthed (orduriers) talked like the imitation of Christ. Finally there was a brazen utopian, who asserted that the greatest pleasure of love would be for citizens to form their country.

Moi, je dis: la volupte unique supreme et de l'amour git dans la certitude de faire le mal. Et l'homme et la femme savent, de naissance, que dans le mal se trouve toute volupte.

11 [175]

We love women in relation to, as they are foreign to us. Aimer les femmes intelligent est un plaisir de pederast.

11 [176]

Leanness is naked, indecente as fat.

11 [177]

Enthousiasme qui a l'autre chose que les s'applique abstractions est un signe de faiblesse et de maladie.

11 [178]

The prayer. Connais done d'une vie apres les Jouissance et prie, sans Cesse prie. Est la priere reservoir de force.

11 [179]

The peoples do anything to have no great men. The great man must, therefore, to exist in order to have a force in the attack, which is larger than the resistive force that is developed through millions of individuals.

11 [180]

Respect of slumber, sinister aventure de tous les Soir, one can say that people fall asleep with a boldness that would be incomprehensible if one did not know that it comes from the ignorance of the danger.

11 [181]

Say those big beautiful ships, swaying imperceptibly quiet on the water, these powerful vehicles to idle and persuasive expression of homesickness (Heimweh), they are not in a dumb language: "When we depart pour le bonheur?"

11 [182]

En politique sur le vrai celui est, qui et fouette do le peuple, pour le bien du peuple.

11 [183]

The beauty, as you understand it Baudelaire (and Richard Wagner -) Slightly glowing and sad, a little uncertain, giving room for the supposition.

11 [184]

une tete seduisante et belle, une tete de femme, c'est une tete qui fait rever a la fois, mais d'une maniere confuse, de volupte et de tristesse; qui comporte une idee de melancholie, de lassitude, meme de satiete, — soit une idee contraire, c'est-a-dire une ardeur, un desir de vivre, associes avec une amertume refluante, comme venant de privation ou de desesperance. Le mystere, le regret sont aussi des caracteres du Beau.

11 [185]

A beautiful head man has no need to include (except perhaps in the eyes of a woman), this idea of pleasure in itself, which, in a white faced (Weibsgesicht), so as to attract one more provocation than it is generally melancholic. But this head glowing something sad and will contain, of spiritual needs, of aspirations that are kept in the dark, the idea of a power that gronde et basically not used, sometimes the idea d'une insensibilite vengeresse, sometimes - in the most interesting case - the mystery and finally le malheur.

11 [186]

Auto-idolatry. Poetic harmony of character. Eurythmy of the character and abilities. Retain all the skills. All abilities do grow. A cult.

11 [187]

What fascinates and makes up the beauty in woman.

fair blase, fair ennuye, l'air evapore, fair impudent, fair froid, regarder de l'air en dedans, l'air de domination, fair de volonte, fair mechant, fair malade, l'air chat, enfantillage, et nonchalance malice Mele.

11 [188]

In Protestant countries lack two things that are indispensabel for the happiness of a wellbred man, la galanterie et la devotion

11 [189]

Exhilarating at the bad taste: the aristocratic pleasure of displeasing.

11 [190]

The Stoicism, which has only a sacrament: a suicide...

11 [191]

La femme est naturelle, c'est-a-dire abominable. Aussi est-elle toujours vulgaire, c'est-adire le contraire du dandy.

11 [192]

Il ya dans tout changement d'infame quelque chose a la fois et d'agreable, quelque chose, qui tient demenagement et de l'infidelite you.

11 [193]

il ya des gens qui ne peuvent qu'en s'amuse troupe. Le tout seul vrai heros s'amuse.

11 [194]

One must work, if not taste, at least from despair, because, all things considered, work is less boring than to amuse.

11 [195]

Still quite a child, I felt in my heart 2 contradiktorische feelings: l'horreur de la vie et l'extase de la vie. C'est bien le fait d'un paresseux nerveux.

11 [196]

Baudelaire says of "De Maistre et Edgar Poe taught me see reason"

11 [197]

The death penalty, the result of a mystical idea, which is now entirely uncomprehended. The death penalty has not considered the target company to sauver, material management: they want the offender and saver (Sauver) spiritual element. So that the victim may be complete, must consent and pleasure to be part of the victim. Chloroform, one would be condemned to death for impiety (Gottlosigkeit, <Godlessness>): for that consciousness would take comme victime de sa grandeur and the chances to win paradise, take him.

As for the torture, it comes from the infame partie du coeur de l'homme, which has a thirst for lust. Cruaute et volupte identical sensations, such as extreme heat and extreme cold.

11 [198]

Ce qu'il ya de vil dans une fonction quelconque.

Ne fait rien un dandy. Figurez vous vous un-dandy parlant au peuple, excepte pour le bafouer?

There are only three respectable beings: priest, warrior, poet. Savoir, tuer et creer.

The other people are taillables ou corveables, faits pour l'ecurie, c'est-a-dire pour ce qu'on exercens appeals for the professions.

11 [199]

La femme Sand was a moralist.

- elle le the year he had a style coulant, cher aux bourgeois.

- elle est bete, lourde elle est, elle est bavard. In moral matters the same depth of the sentence, the same delicacy of feeling, like concierges les filles et les entretenu.

- an naive old woman who does not want to leave the boards

- they had persuaded themselves, se fier a son coeur et bon bon sens a son and persuaded other great betes to do it well.

-1 cannot think of that stupid creature, without a shudder of disgust (Abscheus).

11 [200]

I'm bored in France, because everyone in it is like Voltaire. Voltaire ou Antipoete (Emerson forgotten him), le roi des Badaud, le prince des superficiels, anti l'artiste, le predicateur of concierges.

11 [201]

Voltaire's mockery of the immortal soul, which, during 9 months, between excrement and urine resides. Baudelaire divined in this localization of "malice une ou une satire de la Providence et contre l'amour, dans le mode de la generation, un signe du Peche originel. En fait, nous ne pouvons faire l'amour qu'avec of organes excrementiels. "

11 [202]

Disinfection of love through the church: marriage

11 [203]

Dandysme. What is the greater man? This is not a specialist. C'est l'homme et de loisir generate d'education. Etre riche et le travail aimer.

11 [204]

It's boring to love: it is a crime where one cannot help but to have one complice (Complicen).

11 [205]

Si tu etais Jesuits et revolutionnaire, vrai comme tout politique doit etre l'ou l'est fatalement...

11 [206]

The dictators are les domestiques du peuple, nothing more, and the fame is the result of adaptation - adaptation l'esprit d'un a la national stupidities

11 [207]

What is love? A desire to go off (hinausgehen).

The human animal is un adorateur. Adorer et c'est se se sacrifier prostitution. Aussi tout amour est-il prostitution.

l'indestructible, eternelle, universelle et ingenieuse ferocite humaine. Liebe zum Blut, l'ivresse du sang, l'ivresse des foules.

11 [208]

NB. Defions-nous du peuple, du bon sens, du coeur de l'inspiration et de l'Evidence. How can you let the women in the church? What a conversation they can lead to

God? L'eternelle Venus (caprice, hysteria, fantaisie) est une des formes seduisantes du diable.

11 [209]

In love, l'entente cordiale is a result of a misunderstanding. Malentendu ce c'est le plaisir. The gap remains unbridged (Die Kluft bleibt uniiberbruckt).

11 [210]

"Soyons mediocre!" Saint-Marc Girardin, from passionate hatred of sublime.

11 [211]

One should not ascribe to the reigning princes of the merits and vices of the people over which they are the masters. These merits and vices are almost always to the atmosphere of the previous government.

Louis the XIV inherits the people of Louis XIII: gloire.

Napoleon inherited the people of the Republic: gloire.

Napoleon inherited the people of Louis-Philippe: deshonneur.

11 [212]

Indelible taste de la prostitution in the heart of man: hence his horreur of loneliness. - Il veut etre deux.

The Genie (Thomme de genie) veut etre un, done solitaire La gloire, c'est un rester, et d'une maniere particuliere se prostitution.

11 [213]

C'est de cette horreur la solitude, le besoin d'moi dans la chair oublier but exterieure, que l'homme appelle besoin d'aimer noble element.

11 [214]

De la necessite de battre les femmes.

11 [215]

The trade is by its nature, Satanic. Le commerce, c'est le pret-rendu, c'est le pret avec le sous-entendu: Rend-plus moi que je ne te donne.

— The spirit of each trade is totally flawed (vicie).

— Le commerce est naturel, il est done infame.

— Says the minimum is accused of all the traders who let us be virtuous, to win much more money than the gates, which are vicious. For the merchant, the decent (Honnetetat) itself is a speculative profit.

— Le commerce est satanique, parce qu'il est une des formes de l'egoism

11 [216]

Only through misunderstandings, all the world is consistent. If, unfortunately, the concepts, one would never understand each other with

A man of spirit that is so, who are ever with someone is to practice it, to love talking to fools and reading bad books. He will draw bitter flavors, which are abundantly compensating him for the fatigue.

11 [217]

One official, a minister - that can be estimable people: mais ils ne sont jamais divins. People with no personality, being without originality, born of the function, ie pour la domesticite publique.

11 [218]

Each newspaper gives the sign of the terrible human perversity: horreur d'un tissu. With this disgusting aperitif accompanied the civilized man, the morning meal. Tout en ce monde, sue le crime: le journal, La Muraille et le visage de l'homme. - How can a pure hand touched without a convulsion of disgust a journal?...

11 [219]

Sans la Charite, je ne suis qu'une cymbale retentissante.

11 [220]

Ont ete mes humiliation of the Grace de Dieu.

11 [221]

Depending n'ai pas encore le plaisir d'un plan connu realise.

11 [222]

Tout est une volonte recul de la substance de parcelle perdue.

11 [223]

as Baudelaire who felt one day on the back stress (hinstreichen) le vent de l'aile de l'imhecillite

11 [224]

Guerir pour tout de, de la Misere de la Maladie et de la melancolie, il ne manque que le travail absolument gout.

11 [225]

"Ridente ferient Ruina" written on his portrait.

11 [226]

1.

That humanity has to solve overall task, as a whole that it ran counter to any one destination, this very obscure and arbitrary idea is still very young. Maybe they will again go before it becomes an "obsession"... It's not a whole, this humanity: it is an inextricable multiplicity of ascending and descending processes of life - it does not have a youth and then a maturity and finally old age. Namely, the layers are mixed up and over each other and in some thousands of years it can still give younger guys a man, as we can prove it today. The decadence on the other hand belongs to all epochs of mankind everywhere there is ejection and decay substances, it is a process of life itself, the resignation of the decline-and-drop structure.

2.

Under the authority of Christian prejudice, there was this question did not: the meaning was the salvation of the individual soul, which was not more or less in duration of humanity into consideration. The best Christians desired that it have an end as soon as possible: - about what the individual do needful, there was no doubt... The task was now to individuals, as in any future for a future husband: the value, meaning, the radius value was determined, absolutely, eternally one with God... That which deviated from this eternal type was sinful, devilish, condemned...

The emphasis of value for every soul was in itself: salvation or damnation! The salvation of the eternal soul! Extreme form of self-concentration (Verselbstung)... For every soul there was only one perfection, but one ideal, but one way to salvation... most extreme form of equality, builds on an optical magnification of his own importance to the nonsensical... Nothing but nonsense important souls to themselves with terrible fear shot...

3.

Now no one believes any longer in this absurd-importance: and we have strained our wisdom through a sieve of contempt. Nevertheless, the visual habituation remains unshaken, a value of man in approaching people are looking for an ideal: it basically keeps both the perspective self-concentration (Verselbstung) upright as equality before the ideal. In sum, we believe you know what, in terms of the ideal man, the last desirability is...

This belief is only the result of an immense indulgence by the Christian ideal: as one which, with careful examination of each of the "ideal type", once again pulling out. It is believed to know, firstly, that the approach is desirable in a type; to know, secondly, the nature of this type is, thirdly, that any deviation from this type of a decrease, inhibition, a force and power loss of the people... states, where has this perfect dream man the vast majority of numbers for themselves: there are higher and our socialists, even the men utilitarians, not taken. - This seems a goal in the development of mankind to come: at any rate is the belief in the ideal of progress is the only form in which thought is a kind of goal in the history of mankind today. In summa: we have the arrival of the "kingdom of God" moved into the future, on the earth in's human - but it has been basically kept the faith in the old ideal...

11 [227]

To understand:

That every species has contributed decay and disease constantly to produce the total value-judgments: that the ruling has become value-judgments decadence even comes to obesity, that we have to fight not only against the sequelae of all current misery of degeneration, but all previous decadence backward that is (d.h.) has remained alive. Such an aberration-overall area of mankind from its basic instincts, such decadenceoverall of value judgments is the question mark par excellence, the real enigma that abandons the animal "man" the philosopher -

11 [228]

The main types of pessimism, the pessimism of the sensitivity (the hyperexcitability with a preponderance of the feelings of pain (die Uberreizbarkeit mit einem Ubergewicht der Unlustgefiihle))

The pessimism of the "unfree will" (in other words, the lack of inhibition against the forces of stimuli)

The pessimism of the doubt (: the fear of all parties, especially touch and mixing) the associated psychological states can be observed in overall (allesammt) madhouse, even if in a certain exaggeration. Ditto the "nihilism" (by the nagging feeling of "nothing (Nichts) "

But where is the Pascal's moral pessimism?

the metaphysical pessimism of the Vedanta philosophy?

the social pessimism of the anarchists (or Shelley's)?

the compassion-pessimism (like Tolstoy's, Alfred de Vigny's)?

- are not all equally decay and morbidity phenomena? The excessive... Important business of moral-values, or "beyond" fictions, or social calamities and sufferings of all: each such exaggeration of a single viewpoint is in itself a sign of disease. Likewise, the preponderance of the No on the Yes!

What is not to be confused here: the desire to say no and do-no (Neinthun) a tremendous force and power of affirmation - all peculiarly rich and powerful people and times. A luxury to speak, a form of courage too, which opposes the terrible, a sympathy for the terrible and questionable, because, among other things, terrible and questionable: the Dionysian in will, spirit, flavor.

11 [229]

Leopardi complains, has reason to complain: but that he does not belong to the perfect type of the nihilists.

11 [230]

J'ecris pour une d'Dizains ames que je ne peut-etre verrai jamais, mais que j'adore les sans avoir vues. Stendhal.

11 [231]

1844 c. Baudelaire depending on Sainte-Beuve (Joseph Delorme) says... SainteBeuve says to him: "Vous dites vrai, ma se poesie rattache a la votre. J'avais gout du meme fruit amer, plein de cendres, au fond. "

11 [232]

Baudelaire: ("Volupte" l'histoire d'Amaury)

et devant le Miroir, j'ai Perfectionn l'art cruel, qu'une demon, en naissant, m'a donne, — de la douleur pour faire une vraie volupte, son d'ensanglanter times plaie et de gratter Sat

11 [233]

Concevoir canevas un pour une lyrique buffoonery - translate et cela en un roman serieux. Noyer le tout dans une et atmosphere abnormal songeuse, - dans des grands jours atmosphere - Que ce soit quelque chose de meme de serein bcnjant et dans la passion. Regions de la poesie pure.

11 [234]

The further development of mankind after Baudelaire's idea. Not that we meet again approached the savage state, about the nature of the South American republics Desordre bouffon, where, rifle in hand, looking for his food, among the ruins of our civilization. That would still require a certain vital energy. The mechanism are such Americanization (amerikanisirt), the progress is measured (dermaaBen) the spiritualist game atrophic (atrophiirt) have within us that everything crazy, what has been dreamed of socialists' back, behind the reality remains positive. No religion, no property, no revolution even more. Is not in political institutions, the general ruin show (ou le progres universal: there is little in the name) I have to say necessary, that a few of the policy that remains, se debattra peniblement dans les etreinte generale de l'animalite, and that the political governess will be forced, in order to maintain and create a phantom of order, to take refuge means qui feraient frissonner sonner notre humanite actuelle, pourtant endurcie si! (Haarstraubend!) Then the son flee the family, with 12 years emancipe par sa precocite gloutonne to enrich themselves, to his infamous father to make competition, actionnaire fondateur et d'un journal, diffuses the light, etc. - then even the prostitutes be a ruthless wisdom, condamne qui tout fors l'argent, tout, meme les erreur des sens! Then all that is our virtue as something incredibly ridiculous to be viewed - Everything not is ardeur vers Plutus. Justice will prohibit citizens who do not know their fortunes, etc. avilissement

As for me, which I sometimes feel the ridicule of a prophet in me, I know I never la

Charite d'un medecin'll find it. Lost in this miserable world, coudoye par les foules, I'm like a tired man, who looks backward, looking nothing but desabusement et amertume deep in long years ago and is a storm in which there is nothing new, neither doctrine nor pain. Le soir, ou cet homme a vole la Destinee quelques heures de plaisir - the night that this man is an hour has abgestohlen pleasure the destinies - Berce dans sa digestion, oublieux autant que possible du passe, you are content present et resign a l'avenir, enivre de son sang froid et de son-dandysme, fier de n'etre pas aussi bas que ceux qui passent, il se dit en la contemplant fumee cigare de son: "Que m'importe, ou vont ces consciences "?

11 [235]

A little fresh air! This absurd state of Europe should not take longer! Is there any thought behind this cattle-nationalism (Homvieh-Nationalismus)? Whatever value it might have, now that everything points to greater and common interests, this gruff self incite feelings?... And they call themselves "Christian state"! And near the top circles of the court chaplain, canaille!... And the "new empire", refounded on the consumption test and best despised (bestverachteten) thought that equality of rights and voting rights...

And in a state where the spiritual dependence and denationalization (Entnationalisirung) leaps to the eye and in a mutual self-merging and fertilizing the real value and meaning of the present civilization is!

Econmic (Wirthschaftliche) the unification of Europe is by necessity - and also, in response, the party of peace...

The struggle for a senior in a state that is good for nothing: this culture of big cities, the newspapers, the fever and the "futility"

11 [236]

A party of peace, without sentimentality, which themselves and their children, from using war, forbids to make use of the courts, which the struggle, the opposition, evoking prosecution against him, a party of the oppressed, at least for a time; soon the great party. Antagonistic to the revenge and the after-.

A war party, with the same fundamental nature and severity to be advancing in the opposite direction

11[237]

Buddhism and Christianity: the struggle (Kampf) with resentment.

11 [238]

Abolition of the "punishment". The "compensation" in lieu of all means of violence.

11 [239]

The original Christianity is abolition of the state:

It prohibits

the oath

the military service the courts

the self-defense and defense of any whole

the difference between compatriots and foreigners, similarly, the proper objects The example of Christ: it resists not those who do him harm (prohibiting the defense), he defends not himself, he does more, "he extends his left cheek" (to the question "are you Christ?" he answers "and will from now on, you see, etc.")

— he forbids his disciples defend him, he makes out that he could have help, but will not.

— Christianity is also abolition of the society (Gesellschaft): it's all preference of its outward rammed, it grows out of the disreputable and condemned, the leprosy of any kind, the "sinners", the "tax collectors" and prostitutes, the most stupid people (the "fishermen (Fischern)"), it spumed the rich, the learned, the noble, the virtuous, the "correct power"...

11 [240]

Toward (Zum) psychological problem of Christianity

The driving force remains: the resentment of the popular uprising, the revolt of the underprivileged

(With Buddhism, it is different: he is not bom of a resentment-motion. It fights the same thing, because it spurs to action)

this peace party understands that renunciation is a hostile one in thought and deed, discernment and conservation condition

: herein lies the psychological difficulty which has prevented that they understood Christianity.

The impulse that created it enforces a fundamental fight of its own

Just as peace and innocence-party insurgency that has a chance of success: they must win by the extreme mildness, sweetness, gentleness, their instinct understands that Art: the engine, whose expression is to deny, condemn, take the counterpart of this instinct by deed and word constantly on display

11 [241]

A right to life, to work, to happiness!!!

(Ein Recht auf Dasein, auf Arbeit, auf Gluck!!!)

un reve du doux "docteur charming" - Renan

11 [243]

The Christians have never practiced (praktizirt) the actions, which has prescribed to them Jesus and the brazen talk of "faith" and of "justification by faith" and its supreme and sole importance is only the consequence of the fact that the church is not the courage, still had the will to commit themselves to the works which Jesus demanded.

11 [244]

The Buddhist acts differently than the non-Buddhist; the Christian acts like all the world and has one of the moods and ceremonies of Christianity —

11 [245]

The profound and contemptible hypocrisy of Christianity in Europe: we really do deserve the contempt of the Arabs, Hindus, Chinese... You can hear the speeches of the first German statesman of what has now 40 years of Europe really busy... you hear the language of the court preacher, Tartuffe

11 [246]

— "the Evil" does not resist...

But if you do not believe in good and evil, then what this means? (Aber wenn man nicht an Gut und Bose glaubt, was heiBt dies dann?)

11 [247]

- The old law, which resists evil and evil for evil, and the new rewards that cannot repay, does not resist

11 [248]

- It's only better if you repay all evil by good, - and the person makes no difference

Jesus denies Papal State Society of art, science, culture, civilization

All the sages have so denied at the time the value of culture and the state organization.

Plato, Buddha,

11 [250]

We must destroy this temple and in three days.

11 [251]

I am not an hour of my life been a Christian: I consider everything I've seen, as Christianity, as a contemptible obscurity of words, a real cowardice in the face to all the powers who rule otherwise...

Christians of conscription, the parliamentary vote, the newspaper culture, and between all of "sin" "salvation," "Beyond" death on the cross speaking —: how can you stand in such a dirty business!

11 [252]

You all have not the courage to kill a man or even to whip or even just overwhelmed but the immense madness in the state of the individual, so that it the responsibility for what he does (refusing obedience, oath, etc.)

- Everything a man does in the service of the state goes against his nature...

- similarly, everything he learned in regard to future service in the state, goes against his nature

This is achieved through the division of labor: so that no one has all the responsibility more.

: the legislature and the one who executes the law

: the discipline of teachers and those who have become hard and strict discipline in the The state (Staat) as the organized violence (Gewaltthatigkeit)...

11[253]

That Jesus has said something so dark and mysterious and that there is need of faith, to keep it just as true:

11 [254]

"What is highly esteemed among men is an abomination before God"

11 [255]

The intellectual state of Europe: our barbarity (Barbarei)

the poor and contemptible nonsense of a personal continuance of the individual: a viewpoint on the Hindus, Jews and Chinese are also the faith in God

11 [256]

The entrance into the real life —

- one's personal life saved from death by living life in general

11 [257]

- the church is precisely that against which Jesus preached - and fight against what he taught his disciples

11 [258]

- The mutual intention on the back-paid will want: one of the most insidious forms of value-humiliation of the people. It brings those "equality" with them, which as worthy (abwerthet) the gap distance as immoral...

11 [259]

- you have no right, neither existence, nor work, nor even to "luck": what about the average man, not unlike the lowliest worm.

11 [260]

- "what do, of to believe?" - an absurd question, ("was thun, um zu glauben?")

11 [261]

What is missing in Christianity, which is the observance of all that Christ has commanded to do.

It is the shabby <French: mesquine, petty> life, but with an eye of contempt interpretation (interpretirt)

11 [262]

God made people happy, idle, innocent and immortal: our real life is a false, apostate, sinful existence, a criminal-existence... The suffering, the struggle, work, death can be estimated as objections and question marks against the life, as something unnatural, something that is not to take, against the need to remedy - and has!...

11 [263]

Humanity from Adam until now has been in an abnormal state, God himself has lent his son for the sins of Adam in order to make this abnormal condition is over: the natural character of life is a curse, Christ gives to those who at he believes the normal state: it makes him happy, idle and innocent. - But the earth has not begun to be fruitful without working, the women give birth without pain for children, the disease has not stopped: the believers are so bad here as the most incredulous. Only that man from death and from sin, is freed, claims that do not allow the controller that has claimed the church so certain. "He is free from sin" - not by his actions, not by a rigorosen fight itself, but by the act of salvation freely bought - therefore perfect, innocent, heavenly...

The true life is only a belief (that is (d.h.) a self-delusion, a madness) The whole wrestling fighting true bright and full of darkness being just a bad, bad life: to be redeemed by him is the task.

11 [264]

Religion has forged the concept of life: the science and philosophy has always been the handmaid of the teaching...

Whether one believes in God, in Christ, and to Adam or not we agree that life is merely an illusion, nothing true, reality is

11 [265]

Life is bad: but it does not depend on us to make it better. The change is based on laws which lie outside of us. - The determinism of science and faith in the act of redemption to be on equal ground.

Ditto the fact that they concede to man a right to happiness, that they condemn this scale with the present life

11 [266]

Everyone asks: "Why is not the life the way we want it and when will it be?"

(Alle fragen: „warum ist das Leben nicht so, wie wir es wunschen und wann wird es so sein?").

11[267]

NB. NB. "Man, innocent, idle, immortal, happy" - this conception of the "highest desirability" is to criticize, especially.

Why is the debt, the work of death, suffering (and, Christian talk, the knowledge...) against the highest desirability (Wiinschbarkeit)?

The lazy Christian concepts of "happiness" "innocence," "immortality"

11 [268]

The "peace among men": as the highest conceivable good: the kingdom of God

11 [269]

are at peace with the world considered to no man, when he was a nothing, or how absurd! If peace is violated, does everything, to restore him. The worship of God is totally in the extermination of hostility among the people. Reconciled with one another at the slightest discussion, in order not to lose the peace, which is the true life. What spoils especially the peace? Once the sexual desire: however, monogamy and indeed insoluble. The second temptation is the oath: it draws the people into sin and no one swears an oath under any circumstances, so you have no master over you as a god. The third temptation is the revenge, which is called justice endure the rigors of home and do not give the evil with evil! The fourth temptation is the distinction of fellow countrymen and strangers, with no one break the peace because of your nationality and origin!

The practice of these five commands brought the state to which the human heart desires: among all the other brothers, all at peace with everyone, everyone enjoying the fruits of the earth to its end...

Luc. IV, 18

"The acceptable year of the Lord" - the gracious words which proceeded from his

mouth

11 [270]

the man has a right to nothing, he has commitments for the benefits he has received: he has no one to right. Even if he would give his life, he would not return all that he has received: therefore cannot be Lord be unfair to him. But if a man makes his right to claim the lives, if he pleads with the principle of everything, from whence he has life, it proves only one thing - he does not understand the meaning of life. The people, after they have received a benefit claim, there is something else. The parable of the workers were idle, unhappy that the Lord gives them the greatest happiness of life - work. They take the benefit and are still dissatisfied. You are wrong with their theory of the law come to work, therefore a reward for their work. They do not realize that they have received the highest good for nothing, that they have to show gratitude for it - and do not request a payment. Matth. XX, 1 Luc. 17, 5, 10

The doctrine is the renunciation of the personal life and you ask the personal glory, - a personal reward... In the world there is glory and personal power, you, my students should know that the true meaning of life is not in personal happiness is, but that you serve each and everyone who humbles himself before Christ... does not recommend them to believe: he teaches them the true distinction between good and evil, important and secondary...

Peter understands that teaching is not: hence his lack of faith. The reward is proportional to the work has importance only in terms of personal life. The belief in reward for the work in proportion to the work, is a consequence of the theory of personal life...

11 [271]

Laith cannot come from the trust in his words: he can only come from insight into our situation. He cannot make it by promises of reward and punishment - "move mountains" of the faith can only be based on the awareness of our inevitable shipwreck, when we acceptiren not the salvation that we still open... - life conform to the will of the Lord <Mr.> - (das Leben conform dem Willen des Herrn)

11 [272]

Matth. 21, 18

- In the morning, but when he went back into the city, he hungered. And he saw a fig tree by the roadside and went out and found nothing thereon, but leaves, and said unto him: now grow on you henceforward never a fruit. And the fig tree withered away so soon. And as the disciples saw it, they marveled, saying: how did the fig tree withered but so soon?

11 [273]

The five commands: you angry not, do not commit adultery; does not swear; defend yourselves not by force, does not draw into the war: You can, at moments, missing from these statutes, as you now to the articles of the code civil and mondain code missing. But, in moments of calm, then you will not do what it does now: you will not you organize an existence, which makes the task so difficult, not to be angry, not to break the marriage, not to swear not to to defend by force, not to go to war. Organized, you do rather an existence that it would make you hard to this!

11 [274]

For this your present life - Tolstoy says to the unbelievers, to us philosophers vous n'avez actuellement aucune regie, drink celles qui sont Written on par des hommes que vous et mises en vigueur n'estimez pas par la police. La doctrine de Jesus vous donne ces regies, qui, assurement, sont d'accord avec votre loi, loi de votre parceque T altruism 'ou de la volonte unique n'est pas autre chose qu'une mauvaise paraphrase de cette meme doctrine de Jesus.

Tolstoy, ma religion. Moscow, January 22, 1884

11 [275]

No God died for our sins, no salvation through faith, no resurrection after death these are all false mints of the real Christianity, for which one must make that sinister cross-head is responsible;

The good life is to love and humility, in the heart, fullness, which excludes even the lowliest not, in the formal renunciation of the reserve law—like, on defense, to victory in the sense of personal triumph, believing in the happiness here on earth, despite distress, resistance, and death; in forgiveness, in the absence of anger, contempt, do not want to be rewarded, no one, have merged, and the religious-spiritual of ownerless, a very proud life under the will to poor and serving life.

After the church the whole of Christian practice had allowed himself to take and quite literally the life in the state, the kind of life, which Jesus had fought and condemned, had sanctioned, they had to put the meaning of Christianity somewhere else: the faith in unbelievable things, etc., in the ceremonial of prayer, worship, hard. The concepts of "sin," "Forgiveness," "punishment," "reward" - all quite insignificant and almost excluded from the first Christianity, now comes to the fore.

A dreadful mishmash of Greek philosophy and Judaism, asceticism, the constant straightening and condemnation (Verurtheilen), the rank order (Rangordnung);

11 [276]

If you do not understand that the Church is not only the caricature of Christianity, but the war against organized Christianity:

11 [277]

Tolstoy, p. 243

"La doctrine de Jesus ne peut pas s contrarie aucune fay on les hommes de notre siecle sur leur maniere d'envisager le monde, elle est d'accord avec leur d'avance Metaphysique, mais elle leur donne ce pas qu'il n'ont, ce qui leur est ce qu'il cherchent et ADDITION: elle leur donne le chemin de la vie, non pas un chemin inconnu, mais un chemin et familier a chacun explore. "

P. 236

L'entre les explications de l'antagonism Church, qui passent pour la foi et la foi de notre vraie generation, qui consiste a aux lois sociales et obeir a celle de l'Etat, est dans une phase entre Aigues, et la majorite des gens pour regulator civilis n'a que sa vie la foi dans le sergent de ville et la Gendarmerie. Cette situation serait Epouvantable, si elle etait adjusting completement; com heureusement il ya des gens, les meilleurs de notre epoque, qui ne se contentent pas de cette religion, mais qui ont une foi toute different, relativement a ce que doit etre la vie des hommes. Ces hommes sont comme les plus consider malfaisants, les plus dangereux principalement et le plus de tous les incroyants etres: pourtant ce sont les et de notre temps croyant seuls hommes a la doctrine evangelique, si ce n'est pas dans son ensemble, au moins en partie... Souvent meme il haissent Jesus... On aura le beau et les calomnier persecute, ce sont les seuls, qui ne se soumettent protester Point aux sans ordre du premier venu, par consequent, ce sont les seuls a notre epoque, qui vivent d 'une vie raisonnee, non pas de la vie animale, ce sont les seuls, qui aient Erratum: avent read: aient qui aient de la foi.

11 [278]

NB. It is not enough can have respect for people as soon as it suggests looking at how he fend to endure the circumstances to take advantage, adversary prostrate understands, one sees the other hand on the man, so far as he wants, he is the beast... It is absurd to speak as if he were a hotbed of cowardice, laziness, weakness, mawkishness, humility for the recreation of his strong and manly virtues needed: see the human desirability, his "ideals". The person desiring to recover from the ever-solid value to him of his actions: in nothingness, the absurd, worthless, childish. The spiritual poverty and inventionslessness (Erfindungslosigkeit) is dreadful at this so inventive and informative range of animals. The "ideal" is, as the penalty paid by the person, for the tremendous effort that he has to contest in all the real and urgent tasks. Listen to the reality, so does the dream, fatigue, weakness, "the ideal" is actually a form of dreams, fatigue, weakness and powerless... The strongest natures are the same, if this condition is about them: they deify the cessation of work, struggle, the passion, the tension of opposites, the "reality" in summa... the struggle for knowledge, the difficulty of knowledge

Innocence: they are called the ideal state of stultification <dumbing down, Verdummung>

Bliss: the ideal state of sloth

Love: the ideal state of the herd of prey, the enemy will have no more

so you have everything that made the people humiliated and brought down, into

the ideal.

11 [279]

Jesus turned over a real life, a life in the truth that ordinary life: nothing is further from him than the clumsy nonsense of a "immortalized Peter," an eternal personal continuity. What he opposed, that is the-importance of "person" as he may just want to perpetuate?

Similarly, he fought the hierarchy within the community: he is not some proportion of salary, depending on the promises of power: how can he have meant by punishment and reward in the hereafter!

11 [280]

I cannot stop while the uprising was directed, its author is Jesus: when he is not the uprising against the Jewish church was - church understood exactly in the sense that we understand the word... It was a rebellion against the "good and just, "against the" Holy One of Israel, "against the hierarchy of society - not against the corruption, but against the tyranny of caste, of custom, the formula, the order of privilege, the spiritual pride of Puritanism in the spiritual areas, - it was the disbelief in the "higher men", the word spiritually understood, which led to this outrage, an outrage upon all that is a priest and theologian. But the hierarchy, which was in such a way called into question, was the foundation on which the Jewish people continued to exist at all, the hard-won last chance to remain, the relic of his old political separate existence: an attack on them was an attack on the deepest national instinct, the will of the Jewish self-preservation. This holy anarchist, the common people, the outcasts and "sinners" to protest against the "dominant status" called - with a language that would also lead today in Siberia - was a political criminal, as far as just a political crime under these circumstances, it was still possible. This led him to the cross: the testimony of this is the inscription of the cross: the King of the Jews. It lacks any reason to say with Paul, that Jesus died "for the sins of others,"... he died for his own "sin". Under other conditions found inside, for example in the middle of the Europe of today, would the same kind of person to live to teach as a nihilist, and talking about, and also in this case we would get to hear from his party, her master was for justice and love between man and man died - not in his iniquity, but for our iniquity (now the ruling classes: inasmuch as self-governance already is considered anarchists at fault.)

11 [281]

Paul, with an instinct for the needs of non-Jews who translated those great symbols of the early Christian movement into tangible and unsymbolic: once he made the contrast of true and false life of the contrast between this earthly and heavenly beyond that to which the death of the bridge is (- he put them in the movement of time, as now, and once as -) For this purpose he took a plunge into full paganism and took the personal immortality, something equally as anti-Jewish anti-Christian. But in the world, where there were secret cults, people believed in this continuation, under a prospect of reward and punishment. This gloom of heathenism by the shadow of debt repayment in the hereafter, for it was B., which fought against Epicurus... The trick of Paul, was the belief that Christ has been seen after death (ie, the fact of a collective-hallucination (die Thatsache einer Collektiv-Hallucination)) to exaggerate to a theological logic, such as whether the immortality and the resurrection of the main facts and, as it would be the keystone of the salvation of Jesus order (- it had the whole doctrine and practice of the old town are turned upside down)

This is the humor of the situation, a tragic sense of humor: Paul has just erected in the large scale again, what Christ had abrogated through his life. Finally, when the church is finished, it takes even the existence of state under its sanction...

11 [282]

NB.: A naive approach to a Buddhist peace movement, in the middle of the actual herd of ressentiment out... but by Paul to a pagan mystery doctrine which tolerate finally with the entire state organization learns... and wage war condemned, tortured, swears hates.

Paul goes out of the mystery necessity of the great religious and excited crowd: he seeks a victim, a bloody phantasmagoria, which can withstand the battle with the images of the secret cults: God on the cross, the blood drinking, the unio mystica with the "victim"

he seeks the continued existence (the blessed, atonement continued existence of the individual soul) as a resurrection to bring into causal connection with that sacrifice (after the manner of Dionysus, Mithra, Osiris)

he finds it necessary to bring the concept of guilt and sin in the foreground, not a new practice (as it was Jesus himself, and taught), but a new cult, a new faith, a belief in a miraculous transformation ("salvation" by faith)

He understands the great need of the pagan world and from the facts of life and death of Christ made a completely arbitrary choice, everything is new accented everywhere laid the emphasis on principle... he has annulled the original Christianity...

The assassination of priests and theologians led, thanks to Paul, in a new priesthood and theology - a ruling state, a church

The attack on the excessive-importance of "person" opens in the belief in "eternal person" (in the care's "eternal salvation"...), in the most paradoxical exaggeration of the personal egoism.

You can see what had happened to the death on the cross. When the demon appears bad tidings <Dysangeliums <see Nietzsche's AntiChrisian, #39>) of Paul...

11[283]

That the harmfulness of a people already supposed to be an objection to him!... As if among the major supporters of life would not have the great criminal court!...

We let the animals with our desires untouched, even nature, but the people we want to absolutely different...

The most extraordinary people, assuming that their emergence is a will, a business decision, a vote would have been necessary, would never be striving...

So much I've learned: when the emergence of large and less people would be subject to the approval of the many (included, knew that this, which properties belong to the size and similarly, at whose expense all sizes become) - well, it would never an important human prevents...

That course of action regardless of the consent of the great majority makes its way: it is there that some amazing thing has crept upon the earth...

11 [284]

In Morocco, you will learn about the Middle Ages, in Corsica, the Jewish and Arab history at the time of their concentration; Arabia in the patriarchal age;

11 [285]

Feel stronger - in other words, the joy - always requires a comparison (but not necessarily with others but with himself, in the midst of a state of growth, no one knew that until you compare to what extent -)

— the artificial reinforcement: whether through exciting chemica, whether through exciting mistakes ("delusions")

e.g. the feeling of security, as it has a Christian. He feels strong in his faith may, in its preparedness and patiently allowed: he owes this artificial enhancement of the delusion of a god to be shielded

e.g. the feeling of superiority for example, when the Caliph of Morocco receives only globes, which take on his three united kingdoms 4 / 5 of surface e.g. for example, the feeling of oneness example, if the Europeans imagines that the course of civilization is going on in Europe and when he himself seems to be a kind of abbreviated process of the world, or all of the Christian life at all revolve around the "salvation of man" is doing

It depends on where you feel the pressure, the lack of freedom: depending on where else one of the stronger-feeling created his. A philosopher is, for example middle of the coolest trans rising (transmontansten, <?>) abstraction gym felt like a fish in its waters is: colors and sounds while pressing him to say nothing of the dull desires - from what the other "ideal" call.

11 [286]

Morphology of self-esteem:

First point

A: How far into the feelings of compassion and community, the lower, the preparatory stage are, for the time when the personal self-esteem, the value of the initiative in setting individual is not yet possible

B: How far into the level of collective-self-esteem, pride in the distance of the clan, the feel-inequality (Sich-Ungleich-fiihlen), the aversion to mediation, equality, reconciliation, a school of individual self-reliance is, especially insofar as it forces the individual, the proud to represent the whole... He must speak and act with extreme respect for itself, insofar as it represents the community in person...

Similarly: if the individual can feel as a tool and mouthpiece of the Deity (Gottheit)

C: to what extent these forms of self-denial in fact, give the person an immense importance: far greater use of their powers: religious fear itself condition of the prophet, poet...

D: to what extent the responsibility for the whole thing on individuals a wide view, a strict and terrible hand, a calm and cold and grandeur attracts the attitude and gesture to allowed, which he would not admit to himself his own sake

In summa, the self-collective emotions are the great pre-sovereignty of the staff the distinguished level is the one who makes the inheritance of this exercise

11 [287]

In the concept of power, be it a god (Gottes), be it a man is always both the ability and the ability to use counting to inflict harm. Thus among the Arabs, as among the Hebrews. So with much more advisable to all breeds.

It is a fatal step when the dualistic force on the one of the others to cut... This is the moral to the poisoner of life...

11 [288]

My friends, today we have been on all fours in this "state" crawl and scream like a donkey: it needful, to make the disease knows that one is an ass - the only means to keep themselves uncontaminated by this madness

11 [289]

Heva is the serpent: it stands at the forefront of biblical genealogy (like the snake as a proper name among the Hebrews weight occurs)

11 [290]

The purpose of circumcision is a test of manhood of the first order (a Matura testimony, before being allowed to marry): The Arabs called it "flaying" (Schindung). The scene takes place outdoors: the father and his friends stood around the boy. The tonsor pulls the knife and naked, after he has cut off the foreskin, the penis (pubic portion) along the belly from the navel up to the hips of all races. The young man than swinging a knife with his right hand over the back of tonsor and yells "cut without fear!"

Alas, when the tonsor hesitates and shakes his hand! But the father kills his son on the spot if he screams in pain. Finally the young man agrees to a Deo gloria and goes to the tent, where he falls down in pain on the floor. Some go on to suppuration of the tremendous reason to stay out of ten usually eight left: they have no pecten and covers their belly a pale skin. (In the 'Asir)

11 [291]

uncircumcised barbarian = is both Jewish and Arab (barbarisch = unbeschnitten ist sowohl judisch wie arabisch)

11 [292]

Christianity has not understood the Lord's Supper: the communion of flesh and drink, which transubstantiation (transsubstantiiren) naturally in meat and blood

All community blood community. This is not only inborn, it is also purchased; as well as the blood not only innate, but is also acquired. Anyone who eats and drinks with each other, renewed his blood from the same source, brings the same blood in his veins. A stranger, even an enemy that will divide our meal (without and against our will) result, at least for a while in the community of our flesh and blood taken.

11[293]

Common blood enjoyment is the oldest of the alliance, the covenant. The religious community is society (EBgesellschaft). The animal, which supplies the blood of the covenant, is a victim, and covenant-making is done by each victim.

11 [294]

The "Christianity" has become something fundamentally different from what its founder and that would

it is the great antihelnistic (antiheidnische) movement of antiquity, formulated with the use of life, teaching, and "words" of the founder of Christianity, but in an absolutely arbitrary interpretation according to the scheme due to various needs: translated into the language of all existing underground religions

it is the rise of pessimism, while Jesus wanted to bring peace and happiness of the

Lambs

: and namely, the pessimism of the weak, inferior, the suffering, the oppressed their mortal enemy is 1) power in character, spirit and taste, the "worldliness" 2) the classic "good luck", the elegant frivolity and skepticism, the hard pride, the eccentric debauchery and the cool self-sufficiency of the wise, the Greek subtlety in gesture, and word form - their mortal enemy, the Romans as much as the Greek.

Attempt antihelnistism (Antiheidenthums) to justify itself philosophically and to make possible weather for the ambiguous figures of ancient civilization, especially Plato, these anti-Hellenes and Semites by instinct... Ditto for the stoicism that is essentially the work of Semites (- the "dignity" than rigor, law, virtue as size, self-responsibility, authority, as the highest personal sovereignty - that is Semitic:

the Stoic is an Arab Sheik in Greek diapers wrapped and concepts (Begriffe)

11 [295]

Christianity has implemented from the outset in the symbolic crudities:

1) unlike the "real life" and "wrong" life: misunderstood as "life on this side" and "life beyond"

2) the term "eternal life" in contrast to the transience of human life as a "personal immortality"

3) the brotherhood through shared enjoyment of food and drink according to Hebrew Arabic habit as "the miracle of transubstantiation"

4) the "resurrection" - as an entry in the "real life", as "bom again" - it: a historical contingency that occurs sometime after the death

5) the doctrine (Lehre, <teaching>) of the Son of Man as the "son of God," the living relation between man and God - it: the "second person of the Godhead" - the very carried away: the son relation (SohnverhaltniB) every man to God, even the lowest

6) salvation through faith, namely that there is no other way to sonship of God as taught by Christ practice of life - vice versa in the belief that one has to believe in any miraculous redemption of sin, which is not by man but by that is done the Christ

: it had to be "Christ on the Cross" reinterpreted.

This death was certainly not the main thing in itself... it was just one more sign of how you have to behave against the authorities, and laws in the world - not in warding... That was the model.

Christianity takes the fight only to that already existed against the classical ideal, against the noble religion

In fact, this whole transformation of a translation into the needs and understanding level of the current religious mass: mass of those who believed in Isis, Mithras, Dionysus, the "great mother" and which demanded a religion

1) beyond the hope

2) phantasmagoria of the bloody sacrificial animal, "the mystery"

3) the redemptive act, the sacred legend

4) asceticism, the denial of the world, the superstitious "cleaning"

5) a hierarchy, a form of community education

In short: Christianity adapts itself to the already existing anywhere ingrown antipaganism, to the cults which have been opposed by Epicurus... closer to the religions of the lower mass of women, slaves, not the make-goods.

So we have a misunderstanding:

1) the immortality (Unsterblichkeit) of the person

2) the alleged other world (die angebliche andere Welt)

3) the absurdity of the concept of criminal punishment and the concept of being in the center-interpretation

4) the de-divinization of God's people instead of tearing its obligation, the deepest chasm, from which only a miracle, but the prostration of time helps the deepest

selfloathing

5) the whole world of depraved imagination and morbid emotion, instead of loving silly practice, rather than a Buddhist happiness attainable on earth...

6) a religious order, with priests, theology, worship, sacraments, in short, everything that Jesus of Nazareth had fought

(7) the wonder in everything and everybody, superstition: while the distinguishing mark of Judaism and Christianity to be the oldest antipathy to wonder just its relative rationality

11 [296]

Journal des Goncourt, I.

"A god a l'americaine, who is on a very human way, wearing the glasses through which there is little evidence of the newspapers" - a god (Gott) in photography

... they asked news about your soul "you are in a state of grace?", As if they asked: "have you cold?"

Joubert: missing in his thoughts the French determination. This is neither clear nor franc. This smells like the small Geneva school - Mme Necker, Tracy, Jouffroy. The bad comes from Sainte-Beuve there. Joubert turns the ideas of how you turned boxwood.

- you have from time to time the want encanaillement d'un esprit de l'

- it lacks the broad brush in his conversation; louder pretty small, timid things (of Sainte-Beuve)

- the elderly have been working for a beautiful reality? perhaps they were not a "idealists"?

- they are looking for a zero to ten times its value

- in early youth, when all the vivacity of expansion resigns by loneliness

"It feels like in a synagogue in the East, happy in a religion. A sort of familiarity with God, no prayer in the Christian Church, where one wants to have something always forgive...

The "4 Syndics" of Rembrandt, and the martyrdom of St. Marc by Tintoretto - the best pictures of the world for the Prix Goncourt.

The English comfort a wonderful understanding of the physical well, but a kind of happiness, as it may need blind: the eye finds no satisfaction in it.

NB: rien de si mal ecrit qu'une beau discours.

Flaubert in Salammbo comes to light, swollen, declamatory, melodramatic, thick in love with the color

- the only one who made the discovery of a language with which one can talk about old times: Maurice de Guerin in "Centaur"

-people either love the truth, even the simple: it loves the novel and the charlatan.

It is very strange that the four men plus les purs metier de tout et de tout industrialism, have come les quatre plumes les plus a l'art entierement Voue just before the banks of the police correction elle: Baudelaire, Flaubert and Goncourt les.

We all have increased tenfold in the transport speed: but at the same time a hundredfold the necessity for speed in us...

Tout ce qui est Je hais coeur imprime, you mis sur paper. Gavarni.

A corruption of ancient civilizations, only to feel pleasure in works of man and the oeuvres de Dieu a s'embeter.

we le siecle des chefs-d'oeuvre de l'are irrespect.

happiness in light of Algiers, the flattering type of light: how to breathe serenity...

The melancholy contemporaine French, une Mel non suicidante, non blasphematrice, non desesperee: une tristesse, qui n'est pas sans douceur et ou rit un coin d'irony. Melancholy Hamlet, Lara, Werther, Rene even the melancholy of northern peoples as we are.

The type of 1830: energetic features, mild expression, a soft smile that caresses you; used to the battle of noble battles in glowing sympathies, to the loud approval of a young audience, while the base of the grief and the repentance-supporting, not to comfort, tom heart, have the political ideas of 1848 put him back in an instant fever.

Since then, the boredom and the non-employment of his thoughts and aspirations. Distinguest a spirit of peaceful nostalgia for an ideal in politics, literature, art suffering, complaining, and only a half-whisper to yourself to taking revenge for the vision of the imperfection of things down here.

In the modern code, the code is the honor as well forget la fortune. Pas un mot de l'arbitrage de l'honneur: the duel, etc. What concerns the fortune of today, qui est presque toute exchange operations in the, commission-de, d'agiotage, change de coulisse ou d'agences de, so there is no provision to protect it and defend it: no regulation of de ces trafics journaliers; the tribunals incompetent for all stock market transactions, the exchange agent gives no re§u.

La Bruyere: "On peut se servir of coquins, mais l'usage de doit etre discrete."

How has the courage to speak to a theater audience? The piece is estimated by a mass reunies d'Humanite, une betise agglomeree... (From the book takes you in the solitude of knowledge -)

"If you're good, so cowardly to appear: one must be evil, so that one is for courageous":

a topic for Napoleon III

"Against a good landscape, I feel more a la campagne as an open field and woods in full" We are too civilized, too old, too much in love with the factice artificiel and that we are amused by the green earth and blue of the sky would.

Similarly, Flaubert: horreur on the Rigi.

Literature of the 20th Century and crazy at the same time mathematically, analytically-fantastic: the important things in the foreground, not the essence, abolished the love (even at Balzac the money comes into the foreground): telling more of the story in his head than the heart.

Ces desesperances, ces doutes, non de nous, ni de nos ambitions, mais du moment et des moyens, au lieu de nous abaisser vers les concessions, font en nous, plus entiere, plus intraitable, plus herissee, la conscience litteraire. Et, un instant, nous agitons si nous ne devrions pas penser et ecrire absolument pour nous, laissant a d'autres le bruit, l'editeur, le public. Mais, comine dit Gavarni: on n'est pas parfait.

Journal des Goncourt, I, p. 147th

Cafe a rudimentary condition: for 40 cents. Serenity, perhaps with a gas (gas exhilarant): une demi-tasse de paradis

Gavami: it is cruel, but it is, I have not for two sous in my veneration. (But sensitivity -)

Flaubert: l'idee de la forme nait, highest formula of the school, by Theophile Gautier

il faut comme des hommes a nous une femme Eleveens peu, peu eduquee, qui ne soit que Gaiete esprit et naturel, parce que celle-la et nous nous rejouira charmera ainsi qu'une agreable animal, auquel nous nous Pourron attacher.

The play time, where you can read all men and all women are piano, the world will be in full resolution, they has forgotten a word from the Testament of Cardinal de Richelieu: "ainsi qu'une corps qui en toutes ses yeux auroit of the parties, seroit monstrous, un Etat de meme le seroit, si tout le sujet etoient savants. On y verroit aussi peu d'obeissance et la que l'orgueil presomption y seroient ordinaires. "

No more painters. An army of chercheurs d'idees ingenieuses. De l'esprit de touche non, mais dans le sujet du choix. Literature of the brush.

Raphael has found the classitic type of the Virgin by the completion of the vulgar type - by contrast to the absolute beauty, as she looked in the Exquise le Vinci and the rarity of the type of expression. A sort of very human joy, a round beauty, an almost Junon health. You will remain forever popular.

Voltaire, the last spirit of old France, Diderot, the first of the new. Voltaire was the epic, the fable, the little worn verse, the tragedy to the grave. Diderot has the modern novel, the drama and art criticism inaugurated.

Be a skeptic, to confess the skepticism - a bad way to make its way! The average of the skepticism is the irony, the formula is the least epais aux, aux obtus, sots aux, aux niais, aux is accessible masses? Then choquirt this denial, this doubt at all, the illusions of all, at least, those who affichiren all: the complacency of humanity itself, which requires the satisfaction with it - this peace of the human conscience, which the bourgeois affectation as the peace to issue his personal conscience.

Basically, this metaphysical monologue I feel the preoccupation (Preoccupation) "la la terreur preoccupation et du au-dela de la mort, que les donne aux esprits plus emancipes l'education religieuse."

The man made the woman, inasmuch as he gives her all his poems... Gavarni Clowns and acrobats at their craft their duty: the only two actors, whose talent is unquestioned and absolute, like that of the mathematician or even more comme le saut perilleux. For this it gives a false impression of talent: either you fall or not fall.

Rien de plus charming, de plus que l'esprit fran§ais exquis of Grangers, l'esprit de Galiani, du prince de Ligne, de Henri Heine.

Flaubert: "apres tout le travail, c'est encore le meilleur moyen d'escamoter la vie."

That which struck at Victor Hugo, who has the ambition to apply for a thinker: that is the absence of thought. This is not a thinker, which is a natural being (unnaturalistic says Flaubert) he has the juice of the trees in the veins

De l'amoureux a la mode. Le tenebreux 1830, after Antony's influence. The dominant actor gives the tone for the seduction of love. 1860 it is the farceur (following the example Grassot)

There are no arms to work the land. The education of the workers destroyed the breed, and consequently the agriculture...

gives true freedom for the individual only so long as it is not in a totally civilized society enregimente is: in their possession, it loses the whole of himself, of his estates, of his goodness. The state has, in 1789, devilishly absorbed the rights of everyone, and I wonder whether, under the name of the perfect rule of the state, our reserves in the future, a completely different tyranny, servi par le despotisme d'une bureaucratie fran§aise

11[297]

The half-side efficiency: or the good person.

One attempts to imagine the deity of all the "evil" features and designs equivalent to an attempt to reduziren to half the people who make up his good qualities: it is hurt harm under any circumstances, want to...

The approach here: the intersection of the possibility of hostility, the uprooting of res sentiment, the peace as the one and only approved internal state...

The starting point is entirely ideological: it has "good" and "evil" recognized as a contradiction, it now holds for logical that the good renounced "evil" to the last root and reluctant one means by that, to wholeness, to unit to return to his own inner strength and self-dissolution and anarchy between opposing drives value to make an end.

But it keeps the evil of war - but war and leads!... In other words, one hears much less to hate, to say No, No, to do: for the Christian B. hates the sin (not the sinner holds them apart as holy list) - And it is this false separation of "good" and "evil" is the world of hateful, forever-to-fighting (Ewig-zu-Bekampfenden) has grown tremendously. In practice, sees "the Good" sees himself surrounded by evil, evil in all doable (Thun) - it ends with the evil nature of the people to corrupt, to understand the goodness than grace.

- This creates a cause of hatred and contempt of overloaded type who has the means to cut off but, in fact, war and weapons: a worm-eaten kind of "chosen" apostles of peace

I. The complete "bullhead". (I. Der vollkommene „Homochs".)

The stoic type. Or the perfect bullhead. The strength, self-control, the imperturbable, the inflexibility of a long peace as will - the deep rest of the state of defense, the mountain, the martial distrust - the strength of the principles and the unity of will and respect for the knowledge itself. Hermit type.

The consequent type: here will understand that you hate the evil could not believe that you resist him should not mean that you also should not lead to self-war: that the suffering that such a practice brings with it not only accepts, that it lives entirely in the positive emotions, that the party of the enemy takes in word and deed, that one impoverished by a superfetation the peaceful, kind, forgiving, help and loving states the ground of the other states... that one has need of an ongoing practice

what is achieved here? - The Buddhist type: or, the perfect cow

This position is only possible if there is no moral fanaticism that when evil is not hated by his own sake, but only because it furnishes the way to states, which we do injury (anxiety, work, care, involvement, depending.)

This is the Buddhist standpoint (Standpunkt): there is not hated the sin here is missing the word "sin".

II.

The inconsistent type: leads to war against evil - it is believed that the war is not for a good man to have moral character and consistency, otherwise the war brings with it (and for which he is abhorred as evil) In fact, such a corrupt war against evil much more thoroughly than any hostility from person to person, and usually pushes even "the person" as imaginary opponent at least back in (the devil, the evil spirits, etc.) The hostile attitude, watching, spying against everything that is bad in us and could be bad origin, ends with the most tormented and restless constitution: so that now "miracle," wages, ecstasy, death desirable solution...

The Christian type: or the perfect hypocrite.

11 [298]

How wrong, mendacious as the M were always on the basic facts of their inner world! To have no eyes here, here or open up (aufthun) your mouth

11 [299]

The big words The great men The great days.

11 [300]

"Objectivity" on the philosophers: moral indifferentism against him, blindness to the good and bad consequences: safety in the use of hazardous agents; divine perversity and diversity of character and exploited as an advantage

My profound indifference to me: I want out any advantage from my knowledge and do not move even the disadvantages that they bring with them - this is included what might be called corruption of character, this perspective is out: I manage my character, but think neither to understand him, nor to change it - the calculation of personal virtue is not a moment occurred to me in the head. It seems to me that one closes the gates of knowledge, once one interests himself for his own personal case - or even for the "salvation" of his soul!... One must not take too seriously his morality and not take a modest claim to the contrary, let...

A hereditary monarchy doing (Erbreichthum) a kind of morality is assumed here maybe: one suspects that there is much to waste it and throw out the window, without thereby impoverishing much. Never be tempted to admire "beautiful souls". Know they are always superior. The virtue-monsters with an inward encounter ridicule; deniaiser la vertu - secret pleasure.

Is to roll themselves; no desire "better" or even just "different" are, to interested, not to eject tentacles and networks of any morality for the things

11 [301]

This figure is not of a piece. Not only that they have been faced with all kinds of wisdom-and-upright (Biedermannerei) proverb, so that it is almost vulgar (vulgarisirt) the "moralists": the bad thing is that one has not the type itself untouched. One guesses how

early this character different intentions from the outset has to serve: in a short time it was already just another tradition that already trimmed figure. It seems that the old typical prophet of Israel has rubbed off heavily on this figure: the unevangelical trains, the anger, the curses, the whole so unlikely prophecy of the "court", the whole desert-type, the unrestrained language against Pharisees and scribes, the expulsion from the Temple - the cursing of the fig tree - the typical case, where, and how not to do a miracle

Thou shalt not curse. Thou shalt not do magic. Thou shalt not practice revenge. Thou shalt not lie (- because that one thing, merely because it is held to be true, would have the courtesy to be the truth is a lie: we experience the absurdity demonstratio to three times each day

11 [302]

Here every word symbol, there is basically no longer a reality. The risk is extraordinary, to rob these icons. Cause almost all ecclesiastical terms and value relation (Hungen) mistaken: you cannot misunderstand the New Testament more thoroughly than it has misunderstood the church. They was missing all the prerequisites to understanding: the historian-neutrality, which takes care of the devil is whether "the salvation of the soul" in the words depends

The church has never had the good will to understand the New Testament: they wanted to prove to him. They sought and always look the same a theological system: it requires, - they believes in the one truth. It took until the nineteenth century - le siecle de l'irrespect - some of the preliminary conditions to win back to the book as a book (rather than truth) to read about this story is not as "sacred history", but as a of devilry fable, grooming, forgery, palimpsest, confusion, short recognize as reality again...

It shows itself not enough to account for it in terms of barbarism which we Europeans still live.

NB: The fact that you can believe, "the salvation of the soul" depended on a book!... And they tell me, you believe that today.

What helps all scientific education, all criticism and hermeneutics, if such a paradox of biblical interpretation, as it keeps the Church maintains, did not blush to the body color?

11 [303]

Dear

Look into it: this love, this compassion of the women - there is something selfish?... And if they sacrifice themselves, their honor, their reputations, who sacrifice themselves? the man? or rather a rampant needs?

- these are just as selfish desires, whether they do well to cultivate gratitude and others now...

- To what extent such superfetation (Hyperfotation) one of valuing everything else can be sacred!

11 [304]

We would have the right to be choke (chokirt) them: such enthusiasm as the Thekla is something you cannot possibly approve in principle. We can let ourselves be carried away by the talent of the poet used to sympathize with a single individual who experiences it, but he cannot serve as the basis for a general system serve n'aimons et nous en ce qui peut etre France que d'une application universal.

The theater is much rigourous (rigoroser) morality in France than in Germany. Cela tient a ce que les Allemands prennent pour le sentiment de la base morale, tandis que nous pour cette base est la raison. Un sentiment sincere, complet, sans inborn, leur parait, non Seulement excuser ce qu'il inspire, mais l'ennoblir et, si j'ose employer to this expression, le sanctifies. We have much stricter principles, and we never remove ourselves from them in theory. The feeling that disregards a duty seems to us only one more error, we would more easily forgive the interest because the interest lays in his transgressions more skill and decency. The feeling is challenging the views, opinion l'brave, and they are irritated, the interest it seeks to deceive by them preserves, and even when they discovered the deception, she knows her gratitude for this kind of homage.

11 [305]

Nous que l'amour comme les n'envisageons Human passions, c'est-a-dire ayant pour effet d'Egares notre raison, ayant pour but de nous procurer of jouissance. B. Constant.

11 [306]

The rule of the units makes the composition very difficult: les elles circonscrivent Tragedies, surtout historiques, dans un espace. - They often force the poet, in the events and characters, the truth of gradation, neglecting the delicacy of the nuances, there are gaps, abrupt transitions.

The French paint only a fact or a passion. They have a need of unity. Ils repoussent tout ce qui ne of caracteres sert pas a faire qu'il la passion ressortir veulent peindre; suppriment ils de la vie de leurs anterieure heros tout ce qui ne pas necessairement s'enchaine au fait qu'il ont choisi.

The French system presents to le sujet qui fait le forme and also la passion, qui est le portable de chaque tragedie, in a perfect isolement. Unity of interest, perspective. The viewer realizes that this is not a historical personage, but un heros factice, creature d'une invention

11 [307]

Need the love of restlessness and anxiety? is it the jealousy as fertilizer necessary? To achieve this it gently into the pure and peaceful air of dreams? - In the other case would be a clever disinterested (desinteressirter) Egoism and the first of the virtues of le plus raisonnable devoirs

11 [308]

Sont les bien peu de chose circonstances, le caractere est tout.

11 [309]

On change de situation, on ne pas se s se corrige deplacant.

11 [310]

The whole notion of rank of passions: as if the rights and standards should be guided by reason, too - while the passions of the abnormal, dangerous, are half brutish (Halbthierische), moreover, their goals by none other than pleasure-desires...

The passion is degraded 1) as if they just un seemly manner, and not always necessary, and the mobile is 2) insofar as it takes something in prospect, which has no great value, a pleasure...

The misunderstanding of passion and reason, as if the latter is a being for himself and not rather a relation (VerhaltniBzustand) of various state passions and desires, and not as if every passion had their fill of reason in itself...

11 [311]

By painting only one passion (and not a whole individual character) gives tragic effects as harm to individual characters, which are always mixed, the unity of impression. But the truth loses. One wonders what would remain of the heroes, if they were not moved by the passion, certainly very little... The characters are innumerable. The theater passions a small number "Polyphontes le tyran ("the tyrant") est un genre: le tyran Richard III un individual"

11 [312]

Future. Against the romance of the great "passion".

To understand, as they would any "classic" taste a quantum refrigeration, lucidity, hardness to include: logic, above all, happiness in spirituality, "three unities" Concentration - esprit against hate feeling, temper, hatred of the multiple, uncertain, tail end, just as well against the unsuspecting Short Lace Pretty Kind (Kurze Spitze Hiibsche Giitige)

One should not play with artistic formulas: one should remodel the life that it must formulate afterwards...

It is a cheerful comedy, only now we laugh about the learning that we see only now, that the contemporaries of Herder, Winckelmann, Goethe and Hegel were claimed to have discovered the classical ideal again... And at the same time Shakespeare!

- and the same sex had broken away from the classical school of French in vile

sort!

- as if not of the essence here as good as could be learned from there!...

But they wanted the "nature", the "naturalness": oh stupidity! it was believed that classicism is a kind of naturalness!

Cannot think without prejudice and softness to an end, which grow on the ground a classic taste.

Induration, simplification, strengthening, change for the worst (Verboserung) of man: it belongs together. The logical and psychological simplification. The contempt of the details of the complex, the unknown

The Romantics in Germany protested against the non-Classicism, but rather against reason, intelligence, taste, 18 Century.

The sensitivity of the romantic-Wagnerian music: unlike the classic sensibility... the will to unity (because the unit tyrannised: namely, the listeners, viewers) but unable to let it tyrannize in the main: namely in regard to the work itself (on the renunciation, shortening, clarify, simplify.

overwhelmed by the mass (Wagner, Victor Hugo, Zola, Taine) and never with the size (und nie mit der GroBe)

11 [313]

"Fancied you think I should hate life, flee into deserts, because not all ripen flowers dream (Bluthentraume)?" - says the Prometheus of Goethe.

11 [314]

Wagner's art: a compromise between the three modem needs: for morbidity, according to brutal and innocent (idiot)...

11 [315]

Why the German music culminates at the time of German Romanticism? Why Goethe is missing in the German music? How much Schiller, precisely how much "Thekla" in contrast, is Beethoven!

- Schumann Eichendorff, Uhland, Heine, Hoffmann, Tieck in itself

- Richard Wagner Freischutz, Hoffmann, Grimm, the romantic saga, the mystical Catholicism of instinct, symbolism, the "free-thinking and the Restless" has, Rousseau's intentions

The "Flying Dutchman" tastes like France, where le tenebreux 1830, the seducer-type was

- Worship of the music: the revolutionary romanticism of the form Wagner says (resumirt) the romance, the German and French

11 [316]

The great words: "Peace of Soul" the "love" the "classical taste"

11 [317]

The nationalism has in France as in Germany spoiled the spirit and flavor: a major defeat - and a definitive - to endure, one must be younger and healthier than the winner

11 [318]

The exoticism among the followers of Wagner's "Germanising" (Der Exotism Wagners unter den Anhangem der "Deutschthumelei")

11 [319]

The humor of European culture: it thinks this is true, but that does such Example, what use all the arts of reading and criticism when the church interpretation of the Bible (the Protestant as well as Catholic) will still receive up!

11 [320]

The Wagnerian, with his hasty admiration for everything to Wagner is not at all wonderful, but "Wagnerian"

11 [321]

- this absurd overload with details, these underscore the small trains, the mosaic effect: Paul Bourget

The ambition of the grand style - and non-renunciation want-for what he did better on the small, the smallest, this overloading with details, this chaser working in moments where no one should have small eyes, this restlessness the eye, which will soon be set for mosaic and soon tossed for daring wall frescoes

I have the peculiar agony that excites me, listening to music Wagn, to back out, that this music is like a painting that does not allow me to stay in one place... that the eye continually to understand, adapt differently must: myopic soon, so it the most refined mosaic chaser working (Ciseleurarbeit) not miss, sometimes for bold and brutal frescoes, which will be seen from very far away. The non-cling-can make a certain look from the style of Wagner's music: style used here in the sense of style disabilities

11 [322]

Wagner: 1) do not be fooled by the German tendency

- his sensibility is so little German as possible, however, so his German kind of spirit and spirituality (counting style)

- he has the deepest sympathy for the great symbols of medieval Europe, and explores its "carrier"

- the type of his hero is so little German as possible: Tannhauser, The Flying

Dutchman, Rienzi, Lohengrin, Elsa, Tristan, Siegfried, Parsifal: they try but the :

remains of the "Meistersinger"

- the worship of the "passion" is not German

- the worship of the "drama" is not German: he has tremendous powers of persuasion through force and terror of the gesture.

2) what is German?

- the uncertainty of symbolism, the desire to inaccurate thought, the wrong "profundity", the arbitrary, the lack of fire, wit and grace, the inability to great line in the necessaries

3) one must in the main not be misled: the musical drama W is a step backward, worse, a decadent form of music

- he has everything musical, the music offered to make them an art of expression, the gain, the suggestion of psychological and picturesque

the extraordinary actor and theatrical instincts had been similarly, not German (you know nothing about Wagner, if you're not in this his faculte martresse instinct, his dominant instinct understands)

the German depth, multiplicity, arbitrariness, abundance, uncertainty: the great symbols and enigmas, with gentle thunder of tremendous distance louder: the German gray skies and evil, who knows happiness only as caricature and desire

11[323]

Where he gets his appendix? For the majority of the unmusical, musical half, three-quarter-educated people of both sexes, whose vanity is flattered to understand Wagner

Victory of the non-musical, half musical education enthusiast, the flatter the great Wagner's attitude, as if there was a sign of superiority, to "understand" here : he appeals to the good feelings and the advanced breast he particularly excited what a rapturous - the German - Natural sensation (Naturempfindung)

- he hypnotized the mystical-erotic females, by his music in the spirit of a

mesmerist to their spinal cord inside makes palpable (- to watch the Lohengrin prelude in its physiological effects on secretion and

- every time he reached the height of pathos at the same time with a width and current expansion, which puts him in contrast to all short of breath and moment dramatists

11 [324]

the misunderstandings of the Church the Last Supper "The Son of God"

the death on the cross as a redemption the fall-story of "faith"

11 [325]

For a critique of the good man

Rectitude, dignity, sense of duty, justice, humanity, honesty, uprightness, good conscience - these are really fine-sounding words, properties for its own sake in the affirmative and approved? or are brought here to be worth indifferent (werthindifferente) properties and states only under any aspect, where they have value? - If the value of these qualities in them or in the benefit, advantage that follows from them (it seems to follow to follow, is expected)?

I do not mean, of course, an opposition between ego and alter in judging: the question is whether the consequences are, it is for the wearer of these properties, whether for the environment, society, the "humanity" in respect of which these properties are worth will: or if they have value in themselves...

Put another way: it is the utility, which condemn the opposite qualities, denying fight, called (- unreliability, duplicity, crankiness, self-uncertainty, inhumanity -)? Is the nature of such properties or only the consequence of such properties condemned?

In other words, it would be desirable that human existed not this second property? - This at least is believed

But here lies the error, the shortsightedness, the narrowness of the angle-egoism.

In other words, it would be desirable to create conditions in which the whole advantage on the side of the righteous is - so that the opposite natures and instincts were discouraged and slowly die out?

- This is basically a question of taste and aesthetics: it would be desirable that the "most honorable" i.e. most boring man species would be left? the rectangular, the virtuous, the worthies, the brave, the lines, the "idiots"?

- Considering the vast profusion of "others" away: thus even the righteous do not even have a right to existence: he is no longer necessary - and we realize that only the gross utility has brought such an insufferable virtue in honor.

The desirability is perhaps on the reverse side: to create conditions that is where the "righteous man" in the humble position of a "useful tool" depressed - as the "perfect herd animal," at best herd herdsman: in short, where he not to be more in the upper order is coming -: what other properties requested

11 [326] Rubrics.

1 For a critique of the "good people".

2 From the School of the strong.

3 The three big words.

4 For a critique of "Christian".

5 How can virtue to rule brings.

6 The aesthetic value, its origin and future.

7 The advent of nihilism.

8 For the "modernity"

11 [327]

Diary of the Nihilist... discovered the thrill of the "falsity" "blank" no more thoughts, and the strong emotions revolving around objects without value:

- Audience for these absurd movements for and against

- superior, sneering, cold against the

- the strongest impulses appear as liars, as if we should believe in their objects, as if to tempt us

- the strongest force cannot remember what for?

- it's all there, but no use

atheism as the ideallessness (Ideallosigkeit) phase rejected it, and the passionate no-doing (Neinthuns): it discharges itself into the accumulated desire for affirmation, for worship... phase of contempt themselves against the no...

even against the doubt... themselves against the irony... himself against the contempt...

Disaster: if the lie is not something divine...

if not the value of all things lies in the fact that they are wrong?... if not merely the result of the desperation of a belief in the divinity (Gottheit) of truth

if not just the lies and make false (falsification), the sense-inserting one value, a meaning, a purpose

if one should not believe in God, not because it is true (but rather false because he -?

11 [328]

I.

Concept of nihilism.

On the psychology of the nihilists. The History of European Nihilism Critique of "modernity"

The big words.

From the School of the strong.

The good man.

The Christianity

Genealogy of the ideal

The circle (Circe) of philosophers The aesthetic values: origin and criticism

Art and Artists: New question mark.

11 [329]

NB. Critique of fatherland (Vaterlanderei) (to "modernity").

11 [330]

Winckelmann and Goethe's Greeks, Victor Hugo's Orientals, Wagner's EddaPerson (Edda-Personnagen) gnawing, W. Scott English of the 13th Century - at some point you will discover the whole comedy: it was all beyond measure historically wrong, but - modern, true!

11 [331]

Besi.

Accuse anyone

My wishes have not enough strength to guide me

themselves against these negateurs jealous: jealous of their hopes - that they can take a hatred so serious!

"Why use this power?"

With them to join me, because I did not prevent the fear of ridicule - and I'm out - but the hatred and contempt they inspire me. I have, despite everything faut, the habits of an homme comme il, and its traffic is repugnant to me.

"If I had more hate and jealousy in regard to perceived them, maybe I would have sat down with them into the agreement."

"I have fear of suicide, because I'm afraid to show size of the soul... I see that this would be another tromperie, - one last lie to all the myriad of yore! - What advantage is there in it, self-deception, only to play the Grand? -1 always indignation and shame was a stranger I'll never know the despair... "

Also note that I have no pity for you to call, and you do not guess you expect to... Meanwhile, I'll call you and you expect

I can, as I have always been able to have the want to do a good deed and I have pleasure in; way but I also wish to do evil and I also satisfaction there. All these impressions, if they occur at all, which is rare enough, as always, very easy...

"On peut traverser sur une une riviere poutre et non sur un Copeau." I have exhausted debauchery experiment on a grand scale, and my strength here, but I do not love her, she was not my goal.

If you no longer attached to his country, one has no more gods, which means no more destinations in existence...

One can endlessly diskutiren about everything, but for me is only a negation of any size and without force emerged. Finally, I still flatter myself by talking sun everything is always faible et mou.

The generous Kirilov has been defeated by one thought: he shot himself. I see the greatness of his soul in that he has lost his head. I would never act so. I never would have believed in an idea so passionately... More than that, it is impossible for me to occupy myself with ideas to such a point... Never, never would I be able to shoot me...

I know that I should kill myself, that I should cleanse the earth of mine, how miserable of an insect.

11 [332]

On the psychology of the nihilists.

"The most venerable of men, according to Goethe: consistency, which is one

of the nihilists.

Around this time he persuades himself to debauchery. One should not underestimate the logic is not, one must philosopher to understand. The ideas are Tauscherei, the sensations are the ultimate reality... It's the last hunger for "truth" of the debauchery anrath - it could not "love" to be: it must be all the veils and embellishments that fakes wiped therefore it must be the debauchery, the pain and the combination of debauchery and pain.

An increase in: the pain is more real than the air... The affirmative element in the latter has the character of the esteem in which deception and exaggeration...

not the pain (Schmerz) slightly intoxicated, his sobriety... -Beware of the intoxicating and beclouding pain...

—the pain you inflict is more real than the one we suffer

11 [333]

The absolute change, which occurs with the negation of God

We have absolutely no master more about us, the old well value world (Werthungs-Welt) is theological - it is overturned

Shorter: there is no higher authority over us: God could be so far, we are even now God... We must ascribe the attributes that we attributed to God...

11 [334]

The logic of atheism.

If God exists, everything depends on his will and I am nothing except his will. If he does not exist, then everything depends on me, and I must prove my independence

The complete art of suicide to prove his independence

God is necessary, therefore he must exist

But he does not exist

So you cannot live anymore.

This idea has also consumed Stavrogin: "If he thinks he does not believe that he believes. If he does not believe he does not believe that he does not believe. "

the classical formula for Kirilov's Dostoj

I am obliged to affirm my unbelief, in my opinion there is no more idea than the denial of God. What is the history of mankind? Man has done nothing but invent God in order not to kill. I, as the first bump back the fiction of God...

Another killing - that would be the lowest form of independence, I will reach the highest point of independence

The previous suicides had reasons for it, but I have no reason only, to prove my independence

11 [335]

the beginning of nihilism

the replacement, the break with the floe unhomely begins scary ending

11 [336]

If nature has not spared even its masterpiece when they let Jesus live in the midst of falsehood and a lie (- and he owes the world everything he has let live -) without him, the planet, with all that it is mere folly, now, the planet rests on a lie, a mockery of stupid. Consequently, the laws of nature itself one imposture and a diabolical farce. Why is life so if you're a man?...

"If you are disappointed? if you have to understand that the whole error lay in the faith of the ancient god? "

The salvation of mankind depends on you to prove this idea

I do not know how far can an atheist has to know that there is no God, and has not killed immediately...

"Feel that God is not at the same time and not feel that it's just become so God is an absurdity: otherwise you would not fail to kill themselves. If you feel that you're tzar, and, away to kill them yourself, you will live on the summit of glory...

"I am God only through force and I am unhappy because I am obliged to prove my freedom. All of them are unhappy because they are afraid to prove their freedom. When the man was as yet so unhappy and so poor, so this was because he did not dare to show themselves in the highest sense of the word free because he was satisfied with a student even insubordination... For I am terribly unhappy, for I have terrible fear. Fear is the curse of man

This will save all men and physically transform the next generation, for, judging from me cannot dispense with its present physical form of the old man of God... I am looking for 3 years, the attribute of my divinity: and I've found it - the independence. I want to kill myself to prove my insubordination, and my new terrible freedom

11 [337]

Five, six seconds and no more: because it suddenly feels the presence of eternal harmony. A person can, in his mortal shell that does not endure, and he has to physically transform or die. There is a clear and indisputable sense. You seem to contact with all of

nature and you say, "Yes, this is true" When God created the world, he said at the end of every day: "Yes, this is true, this is good!" This is not emotion, that is joy. Forgives their anything because there is nothing to forgive. You love no more - oh, this feeling is greater than love. This is the most horrible gruesome certainty with which it expresses itself and the joy with which it meets. If it lasted longer, the soul could not endure it, they would disappear - During these five seconds I live a whole human existence, for them I would give my whole life, it would not have paid too dear. In order to endure it longer, one would have to transform them physically. I think the man listens to testify on. Why children, if the goal is reached?

Understanding of the resurrection symbol:

"After the resurrection we will not witness anymore, you'll be like the angels of God" that is, the goal is reached: why children?... In the child expresses the unanswered Fried from the woman...

11 [338]

If people had consistency in the body, they would also have consistency in my head. But their mishmash...

11 [339]

What I like most anger is bom? To see that no one has more courage to think over...

11 [340]

The sign of a great revolt: a cynicism on command, a thirst for scandal aga§ant, irritation lassitude. Unnerved the audience on wrong paths will no longer recognize themselves

In moments of crisis you feel a lot of individuals from the deepest layers of the population appear that no goal, no idea of any kind and have a distinguished only by the love of Desordre. Almost always they are under the drive of the small group of "Avance", which make of them what they want...

The gens de rien got a sudden importance, they loudly criticized all respectable things, they who had not yet dared to open his mouth, and the most talented people they listened in silence, often even with a small smile of approval.

11 [341]

- a criminal seeking solidarity and its hold on him winning?

The espionage. In his system, each member has the eye to the other, the delaware transportation (Delation ist Pflicht) is required. Everyone belongs to all and all to each. All are slaves and equal in slavery. The slander and assassinate in the extreme cases, but everywhere the "equality". For now, the level of scientific culture and the talent to make low, bring down! A scientific level is only accessible to higher intelligences, but there must be no higher intelligence. People of high ability have always possessed the power and have always been despots. You cannot help but be a despot, they have always done more evil than good, they are from exaggerating or they deliver up supplice au. Cicero's tongue cut, fade Copernicus, Shakespeare rocky... slaves must be equal: without despotism there has never been neither liberty nor equality, but may exist in a herd of equality... We must pave the mountains, with low education and science! We have enough for a millennium, but we must organize the obedience, the only thing that is missing in the world. The thirst for study is an aristocratic thirst. With the family or the love of the thirst disappears after property. We will kill this thirst: we will encourage the drunkenness, the noise, the delaware transportation, we are an extravagance propagiren without parallel, we will stifle the genius's in the cradle. "Reduction of all au meme denominateur, perfect equality!"

"We have learned a trade and are honnete people, we have nothing else necessary" - have recently said British workers. The necessary is only necessary that should be the motto of the globe, from now on. But you also have convulsions necessary, we will make sure we have another head and handlebar... The slave masters have. Full obedience, complete depersonalization: but every thirty years will be the signal for convulsions and all will suddenly make them, to devour each other, until, of course, to a certain point, for the sole purpose of not getting bored. Boredom is a feeling aristok, in which socialism there will be no desire. Bookings we us the pain and the desire, the slave will have to socialism... I thought the world to the Pope to deliver. He might with bare feet step out of his palace and the people say, "it has reduce me" - Everything, even the army will bow down at his feet. The Pope above, we have to him and us of socialism... The international agree with the Pope: he will either approve the same, he has no other way out...

They are beautiful! You forget sometimes what it gives to you exquisite! Even bonhomie and simplicity! They undoubtedly suffer, you suffer deeply due to this bonhomie. I am a nihilist, but I love the beauty - je suis nihilist, maize j'aime la beaute. They do not love the nihilists? That which does not love them, these are idols: I love you, I idols and you are mine!

You offend anybody and are generally detested; you consider all people as your equals, and all have fear of you: so is it legal. No one will dare to beat you on the shoulder. You are a terrible aristocrat, and when he comes to democrats, it is the aristocrat charmeur. It is you equally indifferent to sacrifice your life or that of others. You are precise the man whom one finds it necessary...

We urge the people in a self, we've been terribly strong. Not only are our people, who slay, make a fire and make classic coups. This inhibits us more... I do not understand anything without discipline. I counted them all: the teacher who moquirt with the children about their God and their cradle, the lawyer who defends a well-formed assassin who proves that he had a better education than his victim and that he was to get money procure, had no other means, to kill than, the students who try to be a sensation, a farmer kill, and the jurors who acquitted systematically all criminals, and the procurator, who trembles before the tribunal, is not liberal enough to... show under the administration, among the scholars - how many belong to us! (- And they do not know!)... On the other hand, everywhere an immense vanity, a beastly appetite... Do you know how much we thank the famous theories? When I left Russia, made the Littre's theory, which approached the crime of folly, forure, I come back, and there's the crime is no longer a folly, but even the good sense, almost a duty, at the very least a noble protest. "He bien, as an enlightened man is not assassinate, if necessary, he has money?" But that's nothing. The Russian God has given place to drink, all is drunk, the churches are empty... If we are the masters, we are Kuriren it... if necessary, we expelled (relegiren) for 40 years into a Thebaid. But for two generations, the necessary debauchery, one ignoble d, inoui, sale, the needful!... Until now, the Russian people, not in spite of the coarseness of his angervocabulary (Vokabulars), had known the cynism. Do you know that the serf respect more when Turgenjef?... You beat, but he remained faithful to his Gods - and has left the T The people must believe that we all know the goal. We will preach the destruction: this idea is so seductive. We will call the fire to help - and gun shots... II se cache... It takes an incredible force...

11 [342]

The Theatromanie

11 [343]

"Ceci cela Turan"

11 [344]

The Decembrist (Russian uprising of 1825) has sought all his life to danger: the sense of danger he was intoxicated and became a necessity of his nature... The legend of the brave were certainly accessible to a high degree of fear: otherwise it would have been much quieter have transformed the sense of danger and not a necessity in their nature.

But in themselves la poltronnerie defeat, with awareness of this victory and think that nothing could scare them back - has seduced them! Included... the struggle in all its forms, not only in the bear hunting in a duel and he valued himself at the stoicism and strength of character.

But the nervous disposition of the recent sex can no longer be the want of that free and immediate sensations, which with such ardor some restless person gnawing sought

the good old days. N would have been as brave in all cases, such as those Decembrist: only, he would have found no pleasure in this struggle, he would have him with indolence and boredom acceptirt how undergoes an unpleasant necessity. For the anger, it could be compared to nobody: he was cool, calm, reasonable - thus he was worse than any other.

11 [345]

Rome was preaching a Christ who has given in the third temptation, it has stated that he is not an earthly kingdom could do without and has just proclaimed that the Antichrist (Antichrist)...

11 [346]

God as an attribute of nationality

The people that the body (Leib, <flesh>) is God. A nation worthy of the name only as long as she has a stubborn and God are all the other pushes her away (von sich stoBt), so long as it only expects to win with their God and expel the foreign gods from around the world.

The nations will move through the force of an insatiable need to reach the goal: it is the tireless constant affirmation and negation of the existence of their death. "The Spirit of Life", the "river of living water" that aesthetic or moral principle of the philosophers, la "recherche de Dieu." In every nation, at every stage of its existence, is the goal of their movement la recherche de Dieu, a God for himself, to which it believes, the only true. God is the synthetic person of a whole people, as viewed from its beginning to its end. If the cults begin to generalize to the destruction of nationalities is near. If the Gods lose their individual character, they die and with them the peoples. The stronger a nation, the more different their God. It has never been a people without a religion (i.e. without the notion of good and evil) Every nation understands these words to his style. If these ideas are understood in the same way for several people, they die and the difference between good and evil begins to go out and disappear. The reason this has never been able to define, terms, and not even once they separate even close: they has always blended the same shameful in a way: a conclu en la science de la faveur brutal force. This is especially done by the half-science, the greatest curse of the despot, before coming to everything, even science...

11[347]

The Jews have lived only to expect the true God, the Greeks deified nature and the world have their religion that is the philosophy and art inherited. Rome has deified the people in the state.

11 [348]

"Si un grand peuple ne lui seul qu'en Croit pas se trouve la verite, s'il ne se pas seul Croit appel a l'univers ressusciter et a sauver par sa verite, il Cesse immediatement d'etre un grand peuple pour devenir une matiere ethnographic. "

A truly great nation has never satisfied with a secondary role, a self-influential role was not enough, it requires necessarily the first. The nation that dispensed with this conviction, renounces the existence...

11 [349]

il ya la un sens commun au defi audacieux: has seduced you!...

11 [350]

The second half of life consists of the habits that have been contracted in the first.

11 [351]

il faut etre un grand homme pour savoir Resiste au bon sens: un grand homme ou un imbecile.

11 [352]

Malebranche said, God, because he is God, have to deal only with the simplest means "Dieu, parce qu'il etait Dieu, que par les ne pouvait agir voies les plus simples" Consequently - there is no God (Folglich — giebt es keinen Gott).

11 [353]

"His feelings will follow?"

That one, yielding a genetic trap baskets feelings, his life in danger brings, and under the impulse of a moment: this is of little value... and is characterized not even... in the ability to do so are they all the same - and in the determination to exceed the criminal, bandit coarse and we certainly honest (honnete) people...

The next level is, even in this crowd is overcome and the heroic deed not to do on impulse toward, - but cold, reasonable without overflowing the stormy feelings of pleasure while...

The same is true of pity: it must first be sifted through the raison habit, in other cases it is as dangerous as any emotion...

The blind concession to an emotion, very indifferent whether it is a generous (genereuser) and sympathetic or hostile, is the cause of the greatest evils...

The size of the character is not that one does not have these emotions - on the contrary, they have been in the most dreadful degree: but that leads them on the reins... and still no joy in this restraint, but just because...

11 [354]

Christian misunderstandings

The thief on the cross - when the criminal himself who suffers a painful death condemned, "as this Jesus, without revolt, without hostility, kind, faithful, suffers and dies, but it's the right thing": he has the gospel in the affirmative, and thus he is in paradise...

The kingdom of heaven is a state of the heart (- is said of children "for theirs is the kingdom of heaven"), nothing that is "above the earth."

The kingdom of God "is" not arranged chronologically and historically, not by the calendar, something that would one day since the day before and not, but it is a "mind change in the individual," something that comes every time and every time is not yet there is...

Moral: the founder of Christianity has had to suffer for it, that he has turned to the lowest stratum of Jewish society and intelligence...

- - they conceives him after the Spirit, which they understood...

- it's a real shame, a history of salvation, a personal God, a personal Saviour to have fabricated out (herausfabrizirt) a personal immortality, and keep all the meanness of the "person" and the "history" left over to have a lesson that all that is personal and historical denies the reality...

The legend of salvation instead of the symbolic and now all-time, here and everywhere, the miracle instead of the psychological symbol

11 [355]

If I understand anything about this great symbolist, it is this, that he saw and recognized only inner realities: that the rest of it (all natural, historical, political) understood only as an opportunity to sign and similitude - neither as a reality, as "real world"...

Ditto is the son of man is not a concrete person in history but an "eternal fact", not one time in the caged psychological symbol...

The same is true at last in the highest degree of God again... these typical symbols of the kingdom of God, the "kingdom of heaven"...

the "father" and "son": the latter expresses the entry into those total transfiguration (Gesammtverklarungs) state-of all things, the former is just this...

- and this idea has to be misunderstood to such an extent that it has asked the Amphitryon story (a poorly masked adultery) to the top of the new faith (besides the horrible idea of an Immaculate Conception: as if in itself would be the conception, something stained -)

The deep degeneracy 1) through understanding the historical-want

2) through the miracle-see-like (- as if this was broken and overcome the laws of nature!)

3) –

11 [356]

You cannot misunderstand Christianity more than if one assumes that initially the rough-and wonder-savior-history and that is the spiritual and symbolic corporate-only a later form of metamorphosis is...

Conversely, the history of Christianity is the story of the gradual increasingly coarser misunderstanding, must address one sublime symbolism...: with every extension of Christianity over ever broader and cruder masses, which were the origin instincts of Christianity (fact - which withdrawal (abgiengen) all conditions, it barbarian (barbarisiren) to the wants of the lowest strata of the barbaric later brought with it the necessity, vulgarisiren to Christianity until then...: - to understand -) is a legend in history, a theology, a founding churches came to the fore

The church is the will of the vulgar and barbaric language of Christianity as "the truth" to maintain - and... today!

The Pauline, the Augustinian Platonism - until at last this shameless caricature of philosophy and Rabbinic Judaism is finished, the Christian theology... the degrading constituents of Christianity: the miracle

the hierarchy of souls, the rank order the history of salvation and faith in him... the concept of "sin"

the history of Christianity is the necessity that a belief even as low and vulgar, as will the needs are to be satisfied with him

... think of Luther! What could one do with such gross appetites overloaded nature of the original Christianity!

denaturalization of the Jewish stage: 'waste, unhappiness, repentance, reconciliation "as a left-over scheme - incidentally hatred against the" world "

Jesus goes straight for the state, the "kingdom of heaven" in the heart and cannot find the agent in the observance of the Jewish church - he expects even the reality of Judaism (his compulsion to get it) for nothing, he is clean inside

he just does not care for the rough all (Samtliche) formulas in relations with God: he defends himself against the whole doctrine of repentance and reconciliation, he shows how to live, to feel as "deified" - and how not to penance and contrition for his sins is this: "There is nothing in sin" is his major prejudice (Haupturtheil). To "divine" to be, is the main thing that one has his fill: the extent even of the sinner is better because when the righteous...

Sin, repentance, forgiveness, — that everything belongs to them... that is not mixed into Judaism, or it is pagan

11 [357]

the deep instinct for how they should live to be "in heaven" feeling, while in other cases not at all feel in heaven... that is the psychological reality of Christianity

11 [358]

Our nineteenth century finally has the prerequisite for understanding something that nineteen centuries have misunderstood the reason - Christianity...

It was unspeakably far from that loving and scrupulous neutrality - state full of sympathy and discipline of the mind - it was in a shameful manner at all times of the church, selfish, blind, pushy, rude, always with the air of submissive adoration

11 [359]

the symbolism of Christianity rests on the Jewish, who had already resolved all of reality (history, nature) in a holy unreality and unnaturalness of the real story... want to see no more - that is not more natural for the success was interested

11 [360]

One is the one who is angry with us, either by deed, nor the heart to resist.

One should recognize no reason to divorce his wife. Maybe: "we should castrate himself."

One should make no difference strangers and locals, foreigners and fellow countrymen.

One should be angry with anybody, we should despise anyone... Give alms in secret - you will not want to get rich

One should not swear - One should not judge - you should reconcile, to forgive you - do not pray in public

Let see your good works, let your light shine! Who will go to heaven? The will of my Father in heaven does...

The "salvation" is not promised: it's there when you live so and so and does:

Not the church is just that: "false prophets in sheep's clothing, but inwardly ravening wolves"?...

"Prophecy, miracles, doable (Wunderthun), devil-expelling - that everything is nothing"...

On a completely absurd way to reward and punishment theory is gets in (hineingemengt): it's all so spoiled.

Ditto is the practice of the first church militant, the apostle and his behavior on a completely erroneous manner as necessary, as shown ahead of fixed...

the subsequent glorification of the actual life and teaching of the first Christians: as if everything would be required... but merely followed...

all the prophets and miracle-attitude, the anger, the evocation of the court is a vile corruption (e.g., Mark. 6, 11 "and those who do not receive you... I tell you truly, there is Sodom and Gomorrah, etc.") the fig tree

"A prophet is not without honor except at home than with his own" is nonsense, the opposite is the truth...

Now even the fulfillment of prophecy: what there is all fake and been rightly

done!

11 [361]

NB. Schopenhauer had come out of his nihilism, a perfect right to be left alone to keep the compassion as a virtue: it is supported by the fact the negation of the will to live is the brightest. Pity, that crosses virtue (caritas), by allowing to live on the weak and depressed and to have offspring, the natural laws of development: it accelerates the decay, it destroys the genre - it negates life. Why does the other animal species get healthy? Because they lack the compassion.

11 [362]

NB. The anti-social tendency, the mental disorder of pessimism: the three typical forms of decadence. Christianity as a religion of decadence, grew up on a floor, which full of degenerates of all three types

11 [363]

We have made the Christian ideal again, it remains to determine its value.

1. What values are negated by the same: what is in the contrast-ideal?

Pride, pathos of distance, the great responsibility of the arrogance, the magnificent animality, the warlike and conquering instincts, the deification of passion, revenge, cunning, anger, lust, of adventure, knowledge...

: the noble ideal is negated: beauty, wisdom, power, glory and danger of the type of man: the goals-setting, the "future" man (- here is the Christianity as is (ergiebt) conclusion of Judaism -)

2. Is it feasible (realisirbar)?

Yes, but climatic conditions... Like the Indian... There is no work... - it detaches from the people, government, culture, community, jurisdiction, it rejected the instruction, the knowledge, education about good manners, purchase, trade off... it will replace everything that makes up the benefits and value of man - it closes it off by an emotional idiosyncrasy - apolitical, anti-nationalist, neither aggressive nor defensive - only possible within the festgeordnetsten <?> state and social life, which these holy parasites can proliferate on overheads...

3. it remains a consequence of the will to pleasure - and continue to do! "Salvation" is seen as something that proves itself that needs no justification, - all the rest (live and let live the way) is only a means to an end...

- But that is thought low: the fear of pain, before the contamination, before the corruption itself as a sufficient motive to let it all go... This is a poor way of thinking... sign of an exhausted race... One should not be deceived ("will like a child ")

- the related natures: Francis of Assisi (neurotic, epileptic, visionary as Jesus)

11 [364]

On the history of Christianity.

Ongoing changes in the milieu: the Christian doctrine, thus changing continually focus of their work...

favoring the lower and little people...

the development of charity...

the type of "Christian" Everything is gradually returned to what he originally negated (in its negation, he was -)

the Christian becomes a citizen, soldier, court personnel, workers, merchant, scholar, theologian, priest, philosopher, farmer, artist, patriot, politician, "prince"... he takes all the action again, which he has sworn off (- the self-defense, the holding court, the penalties, swearing, distinguishing between nation and nation, the low estimate, the anger...)

The whole Christian life is finally exactly the life of the Christ preached the separation...

The church is so good to the triumph of the antichrist, as the modern state, modem nationalism...

The church is the barbarization (Barbarisirung) of Christianity.

About Christianity became master: the New Age (Paul) of Platonism (Augustine), the mystery cults (doctrine of salvation, a symbol of the "cross") asceticism (- hostility against the "nature", "reason", "sense" — Orient...)

11 [365]

it lacks the eccentric notion of "holiness"

"God" and "man" are not tom apart

the "miracle" is missing - it does not exist that sphere...

- the only one that comes into consideration is the "spiritual (i.e. symbolicpsychological) as decadence: a counterpart to the "Epicureismus"... the paradise, according to the Greek term, a "Garden Epicure" it lacks the task in such a life

: it wants nothing...

: a form of "Epicurean gods"

: it is a lack of reason, to set goals yet: to have children... all at once...

Christianity is still possible at any moment... It is bound by none of the impertinent dogmas, which are adorned with his name: it needs neither the doctrine of a personal God, nor of the sin, not of immortality, nor of salvation, yet by faith, it has absolutely no metaphysics necessary, much less the asceticism, much less a Christian "science"...

Now who said "I do not want to be a soldier," "I do not care about the courts,"

"the police services are not taken advantage of me" - which would be a Christian... "I will do nothing to the peace in me itself does: if I have to suffer from it, nothing will get me more peace than suffering "...

The whole Christian doctrine of what is to be believed, the whole Christian "truth" is nothing but lies and deceit and the exact opposite of what has been the beginning of the Christian movement...

the straight, which is in the ecclesiastical sense, the Christian is the anti-Christian (Antichristliche) from the outset: full of things and people instead of symbols, all of history instead of the eternal facts, all formulas, rites, dogmas, instead of a practice of life... Christian is the complete indifference to dogma, worship, priests, church, theology.

The practice of Christianity is no fantasy, no more the practice of the B it is: it is a means to be happy...

11 [366]

Our time is ripe, in a sense (that is decadent), as the Buddha's time was... Therefore, a Christianity without the absurd dogmas is possible... the most disgusting spawn of ancient hybridism The barbarization (Barbarisirung) of Christianity

11 [367]

Christianismi buddhismi et Essentia.

(Comparing the first Buddhism and Christianity of the first)

Buddhism Christianity are religions conclusion: beyond the culture, philosophy, art and the state

A. Together, the struggle against the hostile feelings - this is recognized as a source of evil. The "happiness" as only internally, - indifference to the appearance of happiness and splendor.

Buddhism: to get away from life-philosophical clarity, a high degree of spirituality originated in the middle of the upper classes...

Christianity: wants basically the same (- already "Jewish church" is a decadent phenomenon of life), but, according to a profound lack of culture, without knowing what one wants to hang... consistent with the "happiness" as a goal...

B. as the strongest instincts of life are no longer perceived as pleasurable rather than causes of suffering

propel the extent that these instincts to action (the action is... but as pain) for the Buddhist for the Christians: inasmuch as they give rise to hostility and conflict (the his enemy (Feindsein), the do-but woe as pain, as a disruption of "soul-peace" applies)

(A good soldier has been reversed no enjoyment, except in a righteous war and his enemies want (Feindseinwollen) run.)

11 [368]

The type of Jesus.

It desecrates, if you are a fanatical element into Jesus thinks..."imperieux" Renan

- it lacks all the torture in the belief that it is a good message and the status of a "good ambassador"...

- this belief has not been achieved, has no development, no disaster... but childish... is the childhood resigned in such natures as a disease

- this belief is not angry, not blaming, not punishing, does not fight back

- this belief does not "the sword"... he has no idea that he could separate...

- this belief proves neither by miracle nor by promises to pay... he himself is every moment, his evidence, his reward, his miracles

- formulates this belief is not, because he lives - he has nothing else... for real... "true" ie alive...

- the hazards of high school, reading (the Prophet) to determine its language definitions: the Jewish is the Jewish concept of Christianity, especially the world.

Vehicle, the Jewish psychology, but one should beware of confusing here -: a Christian in India would have used the formulas of the Sankhya philosophy of Lao Tzu in China - it comes to nothing

Christ as a "free spirit": he does nothing out of all parties (word, formula, church law, dogma) "everything is fixed kills..." he only believes in life and life itself - and that is " "no, that is...

: he stands outside of all metaphysics, religion, history, science, psychology,

ethics -: he has never suspected that there are like...

: he speaks only from the heart, from experience: everything else is the meaning of a sign language and an agent —

11 [369]

To the type Jesus.

- What will be deducted? the whole way motivation (Motivirung) the wisdom of Christ similarly,, his life record... the latter should be done in obedience to the promise he fulfilled, he has a scheme of all that which has to do the Messiah to suffer, a program is... On the other hand, each "because "in the mouth of Jesus... Use unevangelical, cunning, wages, penalty...

- What will be entitled to deduct the abundant measure of bile, which has overflowed from the excited state of the first propaganda on the type of their master... they made him their own image, they justify themselves by participating in a judging, quarreling, angry, hating prophet rightly made him... they needed such a "role model" similarly, the belief in the "return" to the "court" (— this is Jewish, s. Apocalypse)

The psychological absurdity and contradiction in the attitude of Jesus against the Jewish clergy and theologians of the Church...

Similarly, in the judge's demeanor in regard to those who do not accept...

Similarly, in the typical story of the fig tree

The psychological problem in terms of the teacher of such a doctrine is exactly "how he behaves with other teaching and teachers?"

His teaching itself has not grown out of the opposition and contradiction: I doubt that such a nature can know about the contrast and opposition to his teaching... It lacks completely the free imagination of otherness-and-want-value (Werthen)... You can to the contrary (gegentheilige) the judgments cannot imagine... Where there is true, they grieve the most intimate sympathy with only a "blind" and not talk about it...

It lacks the dialectic, there is a lack of faith of any provability of teaching, except by the "internal effects" ("fruits", "evidence of strength")

such a teacher cannot argue... he does not understand how one should fight the mistake... he defends is not, not does it attack...

In contrast, explaining, resume, stylization (Subtilisierung), his transfiguration of the old thing ... the shortening...

11 [370]

a nihilistic religion, a senile-tough, all the strong instincts survived sprung-to-do people, and according to - step by step, transferred into other's milieu, and finally in the young, not yet lived to-do people, entering

very strange! a final-shepherd-evening-happiness barbarians, Germans preached! How could all this be barbarian (barbarisirt) only Germanized (germanisirt),! those who had dreamed of a Valhalla... -: the best of luck in war found! - A national religion preached about in a mess inside, not even nations where there were

11 [371]

I: this nihilistic religion studied together the decadent elements and related matters in antiquity, namely:

a) the party of the weak and wayward (MiBrathenen)... (the committee of the ancient world, what she found most powerfully by itself...

the party and the bad moralists (Vermoralisirten) anti-pagan (Antiheidnischen)...

c) the party of the political-weary and indifferent (Romans blase...) the denationalization (Entnationalisirten), where a void was left

d) the party of those who have tired - like the work of an underground conspiracy

11 [372]

Christianity was in antiquity the great nihilistic movement that ended when it triumphed: it reigned and now more...

11 [373]

The two big nihilistic movements: a) Buddhism b) Christianity: the latter has only now reached about civilized states in which it can fulfill its original purpose - a level to which it belongs... where it can be shown inside...

11 [374]

Our priority: we live in the age of comparison (Vergleichung) we can calculate, has been recalculated as never before: we are the self-consciousness of history at all...

We enjoy different, we suffer: the comparison of an outrageous multiples is our instinctive action...

We all understand that we all live, we have no hostile feelings come back... Whether we own it loses out our responsive and almost affectionate curiosity goes boldly to the most dangerous things going on...

"Everything is good '- it costs us effort to deny...

We suffer when we are so unintelligent one party to take a stand against something...

Basically, we meet today at the best scholars, the doctrine of Christ –

11 [375]

For a critique of Greek philosophy

The appearance of the Greek philosopher Socrates a symptom of decadence, and the anti-Hellenic instincts come up on...

Still the whole Hellenic "sophist" is - included Anaxagoras, Democritus, the great Ionian

But as an intermediate form: the polis loses their faith in their egkeit of culture, of their men's rights over each other polis...

we exchange the culture that "the Gods" from, - one loses faith in the sole prerogative of the deus autochthonus...

the good and bad of different origins are mixed: the blurred boundary between good and evil is...

This is the "sophist"

The "philosopher", however, is the reaction: he wants the old virtue...

- he sees the reasons in the decline of institutions, he wants old institutions

- he sees the decline in the decline of authority: he is seeking new authority (trips abroad, in foreign literatures, in exotic religions...)

- he wants the ideal polis, having had the word "polis" to survive (much like the Jews as "people" firmly held, after they had fallen into slavery)

: they interest for all tyrants: they want to restore the virtue of force majeure - Gradually anti hellenish (Achthellenische) everything is blamed for the decline (and Plato is as ungrateful to Homer, tragedy, rhetoric, Pericles, as the prophets of David and Saul)

- The decline of Greece is understood as an objection against the very foundations of Hellenic culture: fundamental error of the philosophers (Grundirrthum der Philosophen)

Conclusion: the Greek world is perishing. Cause: Homer, the myth, the ancient morality, etc.

The development of anti-Hellenic philosopher-value judgments:

: the Egyptian ("life after death" as the court...)

: Semitic (the "dignity of the wise", the "Sheikh"

: the Pythagoreans, the subterranean cults, the silence, the afterlife-fear means; the math: religious appreciation, a kind of traffic with the cosmic all : the priestly, ascetic, transcendent

: the dialectic - 1 think it's a disgusting and pedantic concept collecting (Begriffsklauberei) already in Plato?

Decline of intellectual good taste: one feels the ugliness and all direct dialectic rattling not already.

Together, the two movements of decadence and extremes:

a) the lush, loveable, mischievous, and magnificent art-loving decadence,

b) and the gloom of the religious-moral pathos, self-hardening of the Stoic, the Platonic senses libel, preparing the ground for Christianity...

11 [376]

NB Our most sacred convictions (Uberzeugungen), our unchangeable in respect of the highest values are judgments of our muscles.

11[377]

From J. Wellhausen

Justice as a social requisite:

"The righteousness of the Sermon on the Mount can only get their turn when the civil legal system is self-evident"...

The Jews have the arrogance of a spiritual aristocracy as the foundation on which their artificial construction of theocracy only been possible without the state despised... the state can be no "Church"... The foreign rule maintains the pathos of distance.

the stages of denaturalization:

: by the establishment of the monarchy there was just a nation, a unity, a overall Self-consciousness: but that was the "god of the desert" and also the (Canaanites)

acquired nature god of agriculture and animal husbandry (Baal-Dionysus) The

Festcultus was still a long half-pagan, but was referring more to the fate of the nation and took off his natural character. Javeh to nation and empire in necessary relation: this belief was clear even the worst idolaters: came from no one other victory and salvation. The bourgeois state was the miracle, "the help of God" was "the magistrate Providence," they remained an ideal (- apparently because they lacked...)

Falls as the realm in cleavage and danger, as it continues to live in anarchy and external fragmentation, in fear of the Assyrians, to dream the greater the return of the perfect royal regiment of the national state of independence: this kind of imagination is the prophetic. Isaiah is the highest type, with its so-called Messianic prophecies prophets were critics and satirists, anarchists, basically they had nothing to say, the line was in other hands, they want the restoration of the bourgeois state they wish by no means a "golden age", but a tight and strict regimen, a prince with military and religious instincts, which erects the trust in Jahve again. This is the "Messiah" means any of the modem sovereign longing of the prophets had done enough, maybe even too much: how to be feared...

But it was not fulfilled. You had a choice to give up his old God out of it or something else to do. The latter did for example Elias and Amos: they cut the tape, more precisely the unity of people and God, they not only separated, but they lifted high up one side and pushed the other down: he conceives a new relationship between the two parties, one reconciliation relationship (VersohnungsverhaltniB). Yahweh had been the God of Israel and therefore the god of justice: now he was first and uppermost of the God of righteousness and, apart from it only the God of Israel. The Torah of Yahweh, originally as a helping all his actions, an honesty, pointing the way, solving complicated problems was the epitome of his claims, of which depended his relationship with Israel.

A law was therefore legally, that those to whom it was to give an undertaking to keep it. "Contract" for the law. Initially, the various representatives of the people committed themselves introduced to the attitude of the "Law", now to Yahweh and Israel will be the contracting parties... Since the solemn act by which Josiah the law, came the idea of the covenant between Yahweh and Israel in the middle of the religious reflection. The Babylonian exile has contributed as the Assyrian, that one is familiar with the idea of conditionality, the eventual solution did.

The fall of the empire was the enthusiastic imaginations run wild: the contrast feeling against the rest spreads: is delirious after the exile of a general union of all peoples against the "new Jerusalem". Previously, the national state is the highest desire, now is a universal dream of world domination, which should rise above the ruins of the pagan kingdom in Jerusalem.

The danger was that the Jewish exiles, as before the Samaritan, were absorbed by the Gentiles. They organized the now sacred rest, so he remains, as bearer of the promise and the storms Meanwhile survived...

Not essential equality of the contracting parties: the word berith by the capitulation, the terms of the stronger hangs

Continued: Wellhausen.

Whereupon they could organize? The re-establishment of a real state was impossible, the foreign rule did not allow for such. As showed the importance of institutions.

The old community of King stood at the time of the restoration men in a bad reputation: it was seen rejected by Yahweh... They remembered the Prophet, who said, forts, horses, soldiers, kings, princes - all this helps anything...

The Jewish temple in Jerusalem Empire - under the shadow of royalty, were the priests of Jerusalem grew. The weaker the state, the higher the prestige of the temple, the independent power of the priesthood. Revival of the cult in the seventh century, introducing costly material for as incense, heavy preference for the services (children and atonement) bloody earnest in the exercise of worship

When the Empire collapsed, were priests in the state of the elements exist for organizing the "community". The customs and regulations were there in the main: they were systematized, as a means for producing an organization of the rest...

The "holy constitution of Judaism": the art product... reduced to Israel to be "kingdom of priests and a holy nation". Previously, the natural order of society had their hold on God, faith, and now the City of God should be visibly displayed in an artificial sphere, at least in ordinary people's life. The idea that once permeated the nature, should now have their own holy body. - A superficial contrast between sacred and profane was, off bordered, they urged the natural area even further behind... (resentment active) holiness, empty, antithetical, the reigning idea is: original = divine, now the same priest, spiritually - as is the divine to the mundane, natural, opposed by external features

Hierocracy (Hierocratie)... under adverse conditions with wonder worthy of forever apolitical energy put through (durchgesetztes) art product: the mosaic theocracy, the residuum of a fallen state - it has the requirement to foreign rule. Next Related to the Old Catholic Church, in fact, their mother...

What is the setback was. Yahweh's law meant the Jewish peculiarity, in contrast to the gentiles. This was in fact not in worship: you can find out between Greek and Hebrew rites no significant difference. The worship is pagan in religion of Israel in the priestly code it is the main thing. Is not that a step backwards into paganism? - It is what the prophets have fought most thoroughly. - Also: the cult is by its nature legislation priests are alienated from themselves and overcome. The parties have lost all memory of crop and livestock, they have become historical remembrance days, they deny their origin from nature, they celebrate the foundation of a supernatural religion of mercy and acts of Jehovah. The universally human, the vigorous leisure (Freiwiichsige) walks away, they are statutorily and specifically Israelite... do not pull more of the deity in earthly life, that they partake of its joys and sorrows, they are no more attempts, you do something for good, and they graciously to vote. Nothing but divine grace means that Yahweh has used as sacraments of the hierarchy. They are not based on the intrinsic value of things in a fresh occasions, but the painfully exact order of a will without motive. The bond between cult and sensuality cut. The cult is an exercise of piety, no natural but only a transcendent, incomparable and unangebbare importance. Its main effect of the atonement. Since the exile, the sense of sin is permanent; of Israel rejected God's face...

The full value of the offerings not in themselves, but in obedience to rules, laid the emphasis of the worship him in a strange realm, morality. Sacrifice and offering retreat behind ascetic achievements related to the morality in even simpler connection. Regulations, which originally had mostly the sanctification of priests to worship functions in the eye, were extended to the laity, to observe the commandments of bodily purity was greater by overall importance than the great public worship, and led on a straight path to the ideal of holiness and universal priesthood. The whole life was concentrated in a holy train, was met by always a divine commandment. From the holding, nachzuschweifen our thoughts and heartfelt wishes. This small, constantly participating in private cult (Privatcultus) claim was the feeling of sin in the individual awake and active.

The great pathologist of Judaism is right: the cult has become a means of discipline. The heart he is a stranger: he is no longer rooted in the naive sense: he is dead works, despite all the importance, or perhaps because of embarrassment and conscientiousness. The old ways are patched together into a system, a system that served as a mold, as hard shell in order to save more noble in it. Paganism in its own territories conquered in the cult: the cult is after nature was slain in it, only the shell of a supernatural monotheism - Final (Schluss)

11 [378]

My theory of the type of Jesus.

The type of the "redeemer (Erlosers)" spoiled, yes destroyed...

Causes: the spiritual level, in which continued during all coarsened, moved, shifted, the absolute blindness to himself (- this is not even the beginning has been made of self-knowledge -), the tremendous safety of all dissenters to their master as their apology... to use the criminal-death of Christ as a riddle...

It will be backward in type: the crudity of mind: one does not walk with impunity among fishermen

: generalizing the wrong type of miracle to nondescript (Allerwelt-Mann),

Prophet, Messiah

: the subsequent history and psychology of the young community, which earned their strongest emotions into the image of their master

: the sick and extravagant pampering sense of efficacy (Gefuhlsamkeit) take all reason: so that the Lord will immediately instincts - it's not the smallest trace of spirituality, of discipline and rigor in the spirit of conscientiousness.

What a pity that no one was under Dostoyevsky this society, in fact, heard the whole story best in a Russian novel - morbid, pathetic, individual features of sublime strangeness in the midst of deserts and-dirty vulgarity... (as Mary Magdalene

Only the death, the unexpected ignominious death, only the cross that was saved in general, the canaille, - only this gruesome paradox brought the disciples before the real riddle: "Who was that?", "What was that?"

The shocked and deeply offended feeling of suspicion, it would be such a death, the refutation of a thing, the terrible question mark "why so?" - Because it would all be necessary, meaning, reason, have the highest reason -: the love of a disciple knows no coincidence:

only now came apart, the gap, "who killed him?", "who was the natural enemy?" Answer: the dominant Judaism, its first state

- They felt themselves in revolt against the "order (Ordnung)"

- one behind him Jesus as in revolt against the order

Until then, this war was no train in Jesus more than that, it was impossible for its thinking. Virtually was also his reaction to the condemnation and the death of probably the whole counter: he does not resist, he defends himself not, he asks for them. The words to the thief on the cross mean anything else: if you feel that this is the right thing, not fight-to-not angry, not blame, but suffer, to forgive, pray for those who persecute us and kill: Now, you have the one thing needful, the peace of the soul - then you're in paradise

Apparently they understood not the main thing: the example of this freedom from all resentment:

Again yes the death of Christ does not make sense as the strongest and most powerful model testing his theory has to be...

His disciples were far from all, to forgive his death: the most unevangelical feeling that revenge was on top...

The impossible thing could be over: it takes a "retribution", a "court" (- and nothing less than evangelical reward and punishment!)

Only now the popular expectations of a Messiah came to the fore again: expecting an historic moment, where "the judge" comes to court over his enemies...

: now you only misunderstood the coming of the "kingdom of God" such as prophecy about a final act of the story

: now only it was into all the contempt and bitterness against Pharisees and theologians in the type of the master

: you did not understand the main thing: that just such a death, even the largest margin of victory over the "world" was (on the feelings of hatred, revenge, etc.) - over evil, the evil, this is understood only as an inner psychological reality

: the veneration of these completely out of balance more prudent souls could not bear to believe that a valid equality for everyone "Son of God," as he had Jesus taught: they throat was a riotous manner Jesus uplift (- just like the role of the Jews of Israel had lifted up as if as if the whole rest of the world his enemy. Origin of the absurd theology of one God and his son a

Problem of "how could God allow this?" Then they found the absurd answer, "he gave his only Son for the forgiveness of sins, as the victim." As everything was misunderstood! Nothing is unevangelical than the guilt of the victim and even the innocent for the sins of the guilty;

: But Jesus had abolished the sin! - Not by "faith", but by the sense of divinity,

God equality.

It enters into the type:

a) the doctrine of the court and the Second Coming

b) the doctrine of death as a sacrifice

c) the doctrine of the resurrection, so that the whole "salvation", the whole point of the gospel is eskamotirt at once in favor of a state - "after death"...

Paul, logistic rend rabbinical impudence with this view: "If Christ is not risen from the dead, then our faith is vain"

: did not last the "immortality of the person"

And so you had in the second generation after Jesus already all that as a Christian, which went against the deepest instincts of the evangelical the victim, even the blood of victims, victims of the first fruits Punishment, reward, court...

keep apart from this world and hereafter, from time and eternity a theology rather than a practice, a "belief" rather than a lifestyle a deep and deadly hostility against all non-Christian

all the desperate situation of the missionary has brought into the teaching Jesus all the hard and nasty things, do not accept against which its

missionaries are said to be the champion now been proclaimed Once again in the main court, punishment, reward accepted were back, the whole doctrine and proverb wisdom (Spriichwortweisheit) Jesus was soaked with it...

11 [379]

The nihilist.

The gospel: the message that the lowly and the poor, access to happiness is open that has nothing to do than to break away from the institution, the tradition of paternalism of the upper classes: so far is the emergence of Christianity nothing more than the typical teaching-socialists (typische Socialisten-Lehre).

Possession, acquisition, country, status and rank, tribunals, police, government, church, education, art, military affairs: everything just as many preventions of luck, mistakes, entanglements, devil works, which proclaims the gospel, the court... all typical of the socialist doctrine.

In the background of the riots, the explosion of pent-up revulsion against the "masters", the instinct for how much happiness could be had for so long prints outdoor feel-...

Usually a symptom of the fact that the lower layers have been treated to humane, that they taste a fortune already banned them in your mouth... not the hunger creates revolutions, but that the people have got enmangeant appetite...

11 [380]

The alleged youth

To cheat, if you dream here of a naive and young people's existence, which stands out against an ancient civilization, and it goes to the superstitious, as if in those layers of the lowest nation where Christianity grew and took root, the deeper source emporgesprudelt of life is again: you understand nothing of the psychology of Christianity, if seen as an expression of a new up-coming young people and races gain increases. Rather, it is a typical form of decadence, and the moral temporalization (Verzartlichung) and hysteria has become a tired and aimless, morbid hodgepodge population. This wonderful company, which here gets together for this masterpiece of folk seduction itself is actually one and all Russia into a novel, all nervous diseases, they can provide them a rendezvous... the absence of duties, the instinct that all reason at the end was that nothing more profitable high satisfaction dolce far niente in a

: the power and certainty of future Jewish instinct, the enormity of his tenacious twill to power is in existence and its ruling class, the layers, which elevates the young Christianity, are marked by nothing stronger than the instinct-fatigue. We have had enough: that's one thing - and you're satisfied with them, in itself, for itself - that is the other (das Andre).

11 [381]

Expressing inability to political <add extra letters> otherwise than by religious ideals formulas

11 [382]

Renan.

In the orient, is the fool one priviligirtes beings; before he enters the highest councils, without any one dares to stop him, listening to him, you ask him. This is a creature that is believed closer to God, because, as his individual reason has gone out, assumes that he has in part to the divine. The esprit that singles out a fine scorn any error of reasoning is lacking in Asia.

It has placed less value on these writings as to the oral tradition: and remaining in the first half of the second century. Therefore, few of the authority of these writings: they are tidied, added them, the one (Einen) from the other

In John's gospel lacks the parables, the exorcisms...

11 [383]

Ego:

"I was hungry and you gave me dined - comes from me, ye cursed, etc." Matth. 25, 41, etc.

this outrageous language, "what you have not done one at least of these my brethren, ye have done well not to me"

"the spirit of propaganda," as presents to the mind of Christ...

"the spirit of unsatisfied vindictiveness," which rages in words, curses and prophecies of court scenes...

"the spirit of asceticism" ("keeping the commandments" as a means of discipline, as a way to otherworldly rewards, as in Judaism) instead of that Christian indifferentism, which has all of these commodities by himself, of "bliss"... the essenes, John etc.

"the spirit of sin and feeling the necessity of redemption"

With the death of Christ and the psychological necessity, seeing no end to herein, all the popular tendencies were restored: all the crudities, which in spirit to transform the work that was typical of Spiritualists

: curse of messianism, the coming of the "kingdom of God," the spirit of enmity and revenge, the expectation of the "wage" and the "punishment" of the arrogance of the "elect" (judge them, condemn the idea of victim- Judaism... the socialist tendency in favor of the poor, the "dishonest", the despised)

Jesus, who lived as a popular meeting all expectations, which is nothing other than to say that: "here is the kingdom of heaven", which transformed the crudity of these expectations in mind:

— but was all forgotten with the death (in German: refuted) they had no choice, either the type of back-translated into the popular imagination-the "Messiah," the future "judge" in the struggle of the Prophet -

In the aftermath of this shock, the uncertain and this enthusiastic band was not up, immediately entered the complete degeneration: it was all in vain... an absurd coarsening of all spiritual values and formulas the anarchist instincts against the ruling class come brazenly to the foreground.

: hatred for the rich, the powerful, the scholars - with the "Kingdom of Heaven," with the "peace on earth" was to end: from a psychological reality is a belief, an expectation of an eventually coming reality, "a return ": a life in the imagination is the eternal form of" salvation "- oh how different Jesus was understood!

11 [384]

The first degeneration of Christianity is the impact of Juda (Judain) - a regression to overcome (uberwundene) forms...

11 [385]

"My kingdom is not of this world (Mein Reich ist nicht von dieser Welt)"

"I will destroy the temple of God and edify in three days"

the procedure against the "temptations" (mesith), which represents the religion in question: the stoning was included in the act

- every prophet, every worker of miracles, who removed the people from the old faith "Maitre de ce grand irony"

Renan finds it reasonable that he paid his triumph with his life.

11 [386]

"he's just disputeur when he argues against the Pharisees (Pharisaer), the enemy forces him, as happens almost always, to accept his own sound"

11 [387]

Renan, I, 346

Ses exquises mockery, ses malignant provocations frappaient toujours au coeur. Eternelles stigmata, elles sont dans la plaie restees cages. Nessus de cette tunique ridicule you, que le Juif, the pharisiens fils, en traine lambeaux apres lui depuis dixhuit siecles, divin c'est Jesus, qui l'a tissee avec un artifice. Chefs-d'oeuvre de haute raillerie, se sont ses traits Inscrit en lignes de feu sur la chair de l'hypocrite et du faux submissive. Incomparables traits, traits Dignes d'un fils de Dieu! Un seul Dieu sait tuer de la varietal. Socrate Moliere et la peau ne font qu'effleurer. Celui-ci porte jusqu'au fond of the os le feu et la rage.

And that is the same that could be said of Isaiah 42, 2-3!

11 [388]

He never had a concept of "person", "individual": we is one (man ist eins) if you love each other, if only from the other lives. His students and he were one (Seine Schuler und er waren Eins).

11 [389]

That he is God, God is the same as defamation of the Jews was shown (cf. John V, 18, X, 33). He is less than the Father, the Father has not revealed everything to him. He struggles to be called godlike (gottgleich). He is the Son of God: all of it will be able to (- it is Jewish: the divine sonship of several people in the Old Testament is allotted, of which one pretends (pratendirt) not entirely possible that they are equal to God) "son" in the Semitic languages is a very vague, free term (freier Begriff)

11 [390]

The great Umbrian movement of the XIII. Century, most closely related to that of the Galilean, was in the name of poverty (Armut):

Franz von Assisi: exquisite goodness, his delicate fine and tender communion with the universal life <Nietzsche wrote this mostly in French: Franz von Assisi: exquise bonte, sa communion delicate fine et tendre avec la vie universelle>

11 [391]

in rabbinic language of this time is "heaven" is synonymous (gleichbedeutend) with "God": whose names were avoided.

11 [392]

"The kingdom of God is among us," Fuc. 17, 20

11 [393]

"blessed are God's words and do listen." Fuc. 11, 27 etc.

11 [394]

it is missing altogether, the term "natural," "natural law": everything is morally, "miracle" is nothing "unnatural" (because there is no nature)

11 [395]

"The law is destroyed: he is the one who will destroy it" division among his first pupils, of which a substantial portion was Jewish... The case against him leaves no doubt...

11 [396]

"Neighbor" in the Jewish sense of fellow believer (Glaubensgenosse)

11 [397]

there is no unevangelical (unevangelischeren) type than the scholars of the Greek church, by pushing the IV century Christianity to the way an absurd metaphysics, and similarly, the scholastics of the Latin Middle Ages.

11 [398]

Renan, I, 461

... Que le sentiment Jesus a introduit dans le monde est bien le Notre. Son parfait idealism est la plus haute regie de la vie et detachees vertueuse. Il a le ciel cree ames of pure, ou se trouve ce qu'on demande en vain a la terre, la noblesse parfaite des enfants de Dieu, la saintete accompli, la total abstraction of souillures du monde, la liberte enfin, que la societe real exclut et qui comme une impossibility n'a que dans le toute son amplitude domaine de la pensee. Le grand maitre de ceux dans ce qui se refugient paradis ideal Jesus est encore. Le premier, il a la Proclame royaute de l'esprit: le premier, il a dit au moins par ses actes: "mon royaume n'est pas de ce monde". La Fondation de la religion est bien vraie son oeuvre...

11 [399]

"Christianity" has become synonymous with "religion" all it does outside of the great and good Christian tradition, will be infertile (unfruchtbar <barren>).

11 [400]

Our civilization ruled by a police minutely (minutieuse), gives no idea of what the man does in periods where the originality of each one has more free space.

Nos petites tracasseries preventives, bien plus meurtrieres que les supplices pour les choses de l'esprit, n'existaient pas. Jesus konnte, drei Jahre lang ein Leben fuhren, welches ihn, in unseren Gesellschaften, zwanzig Mai vor das Tribunal gebracht hatte...

Degagees de nos conventions polies, exemptes de T education uniforme, qui nous raffine, mais qui diminue si fort notre individuality, ces ames entieres portaient dans Taction une energie surprenante... Le souffle de Dieu etait libre chez eux; chez nous, il est enchaine par les liens de fer d'une societe mesquine et condamnee a une irremediable mediocrite.

Plagons done au plus haut sommet de la grandeur humaine la personne de Jesus: M. Renan calls on us (fordert uns Herr Renan auf).

11 [401]

The medicine, which in a certain moral delicatesse sees the beginning d'etisie... (de phtisie? (of consumption))

11 [402]

La philosophic ne suffit pas au grand nombre. Il faut lui la saintete. - A like Renan's malice.

11 [403]

Qui mieux etre n'aimerait malade comme comme le Pascal que bien portant vulgaire? Renan.

11 [404]

Qu'on se figure Jesus, tiny room peg jusqu'a soixante soixante-dix to the ou le Fardeau de sa divinite, perdant Sat flame celeste, s'usant peu a peu d'un sous les necessite role Inoui! Renan.

Voue sans reserve idee a son, il ya toute chose subordonne a un tel que l'univers degre n'exista plus pour lui. C'est par cet acces de volonte heroique, qu'il a Conquise le ciel. Il n'ya pas eu d'homme peut-etre Qakia-Mouni excepte, a ce qui ait Point aux pieds foul la famille, les de ce monde Joies, tout soin Temporel... Pour nous enfants etemels, condamne a l'impuissance, inclinons-devant nous ces demi-Gods and! Renan.

11 [405]

Le mouvement democratique le plus exalte, dont Thumanite ait garde le souvenir, agitait depuis longtemps la race juive. La pensee que Dieu est le vengeur du pauvre et du faible contre le riche et le puissant se retrouve a chaque page des ecrits de l'Ancien Testament. L'histoire d'lsrael est de toutes les histoires celle ou Tesprit populaire a le plus constamment domine. Les prophetes, vrais tribuns et, on peut le dire, les plus hardis des tribuns, avaient tonne sans cesse contre les grands et etabli une etroite relation entre les mots de „pauvre, doux, humble, pieux" et de Tautre entre les mots „riche, impie, violent, mechanf'. Sous les Seleucides, les aristocrates ayant presque tous apostasie et passe a Thellenisme, ces associations d'idees ne firent que se fortifier. Le livre d'Henoch contiens des maledictions plus violentes encore que celles de l'Evangile contre le monde, les riches, les puissants. Le nom de „pauvre" (ebion) etait devenu synonyme de „saint", d'„ami de Dieu".

11 [406]

Pierre Loti, Pecheur d'lslande.

11 [407]

The state or organized immorality...

inside: the police, criminal law, estates, commercial, family heart: the will to power, for war, for conquest, for revenge

how it is achieved that does a large amount of things to which the individual would never understand?

by dismemberment of responsibility of command and execution

by the interposition of the virtues of obedience, of duty, patriotism and love of prince

the maintenance of pride, austerity, strength, hatred, revenge, in short all the typical traits that contradict the hero type (Heerdentypus)...

the tricks to actions, measures of, to allow emotions, which, measured individually, are no longer "allowed" - no more "tasty" are

- The art of "making it palatable to us" that allows us to enter into such an "alienated" worlds

- The historian shows their way of law and reason, the trips, the exoticism, the psychology, criminal justice, asylum, criminal, sociology

- The "impersonality" so that we as a media one collective essence (Collektivwesens) we allow these emotions and actions (Judge colleges, judges, citizens, soldiers, ministers, princes, society (Societat), "critics")... gives us the feeling as if we would place a victim...

Maintaining the military state is the last resort, the great tradition it is incorporated, it was noted with regard to the highest type of man, the strong type. And all concepts that perpetuate the hostility and distance ranking of states may appear sanctioned suggest...

for example nationalism, protectionism (Schutzzoll),

the strong type is maintained as a value determinant (wertbestimmend)...

11 [408]

One should not dress up Christianity and decorate (as does this ambiguous M. Renan): it has a strong type death war (Todkrieg) against the man made (es hat einen Todkrieg gegen den starken Typus Mensch gemacht)

it has placed all of the basic instincts of this type in the spell it has fabricated out (herausfabrizirt) from these evil instincts, the evil it the strong man as the typically reprehensible and depraved man it has taken the party all that is weak, lowly, wayward (MiBrathenen)

: it is an ideal out of opposition to the preservation instincts of strong life has been...

: it reason is has corrupted even the most spiritual people, taught by the highest instincts of intellectuality as sinful, as misleading, as temptations to feel...

the most wretched example — the corruption of Pascal, who believed in the corruption of his reason through original sin, while it is corrupted only by his Christianity to him...

11 [409]

To authors, which today have pleasure still, a compromised and for all: Rousseau, Schiller, George Sand, Michelet, Buckle, Carlyle, the imitation (imitation)

11 [410]

NB. I distrust (miBtraue) all systematists and go out of their way. The will to system is a thinker (Denker), at least, something that is compromised, a form of immorality... Maybe one guesses at a glance under and behind this book, which systematists, it is even evaded (Miihe) with difficulty — to myself...

11 [411]

Preface.

1.

Great things require that one of them is silent or talking big: big, that means cynically and with innocence (das heiBt cynisch und mit Unschuld).

2.

What I relate is the history of the next two centuries. I describe what's coming, what can no longer come differently: the advent of nihilism. This story can now be told: for the necessity itself is at work here. This future speaks in a hundred signs, this destiny announces itself everywhere in; for the music of the future all ears are already pricked. Our whole European culture has been moving a long time now, with a tortured tension that is growing from decade to decade, as toward a catastrophe: restlessly, violently, falls, like a stream, wants to reach the end, that no longer reflects that was afraid to reflect.

3.

- The here takes the word has, conversely, nothing yet remember to have done when: as as a philosopher and solitary by instinct, who found his advantage on the sidelines (Abseits), in the outside, in patience, in the delay in the retardation (Zuriickgebliebenheit), as a venture - and - tempter-spirit (Versucher-Geist) who has already lost his way in every labyrinth of the future, as a fortune-telling bird spirit (Wahrsagevogel-Geist) who looks back when he tells what is to come, as the first perfect nihilist of Europe, but the nihilism itself already in be lived to the end, has - of him behind him, beneath him, beside himself (der ihn hinter sich, unter sich, auBer sich hat)...

4.

Because you cannot lay hands on the meaning of the title, with the future this will be nominated gospel (Evangelium). "The will to power. Attempt at a revaluation of all values" — this formula is a counter movement expressed, in intention principle and task: a movement that will succeed in any future that perfect nihilism, which requires him but, logically and psychologically, which is absolutely just can come to him and from him.

For why the advent of nihilism is now necessary? Because our previous values are even there, the draw him into their final conclusion, because of Nihilism intended to end the logic of our great values and ideals - because we are experiencing nihilism only need to figure out what actually the value of these "values"... We have had, sometime, new values necessary...

11 [412]

Read books that could be written by many: they betray most clearly the intellectual habits of the scholar-type of a time (Zeit), they are "impersonal."

11 [413]

The Superman (Der Ubermensch, <overman>)

: it's not my question, what separates the men: but what kind of person elected as higher values (hoherwerthige), wanted to be bred...

Humanity is not a development for the better; represent or higher; or stronger in the sense in which it is believed today: the Europeans of the 19th century, is in their value (Werthe <worth>), far below the European of the Renaissance; development is absolutely no necessity of any increase, increase, gain...

in a different sense, it gives out a continuing success of individual cases in various locations around the world and from diverse cultures, which in fact represents a higher type: something that is in proportion to the overall-humanity a sort of "superman". Such good fortune of great success have always been possible and perhaps always be possible. And even whole tribes, sexes, nations may under certain circumstances such a hit...

From the earliest times of our scenario (errathbaren) Indian, Egyptian and Chinese culture to this day, the higher type of man is much more similar than you think...

We forget how little humanity belongs in a single movement, such as youth, age, extinction are by no terms which belong to them as a whole

We forget to give an example of how our European civilization is only now again approaching that state of philosophical and friability (Miirbigkeit) late culture (Spatcultur), from the emergence of Buddhism is understandable.

If it will one day be possible to draw lines isochronous culture through history, the modern concept of progress will be like to stand on his head - and the index itself, after which it is measured, the democracy

11 [414]

Preface.

* * *

What is good? - All that heightens the feeling of power, the will to power, the power increases, even in humans.

What is bad? - Everything (Alles) that comes out of weakness.

What is happiness? - The feeling that power increases - that resistance is overcome.

Not contentment, but more power, not peace at all, but war; not virtue, but efficiency (virtue in the Renaissance style, virtu, virtue moraline.)

The weak and fail (MiBrathenen) should perish: first principle of society. And they should have to help.

What is more harmful than any vice? - Pity, indeed, with all fail (MiBrathenen) and weak - "Christianity"...

* * *

Not what will replace mankind in the order of nature, is my problem, I hereby make, but rather (sondern) what type of person you want to breed, should, as a more certain future higher, more dignified life.

Higher values (Hoherwerthigere) this type is often already been there: but as a godsend, as an exception - never as deliberate. Rather, he has just been feared most, it has been almost the horror: and out of fear you have wanted the opposite type, bred attained: the domestic animal, the herd animal, the animal of "equal rights", the weak beast man, the "Christians"...

* * *

The will to power.

Attempt at a revaluation of all values.

11[415]

The conception of the world, in which one encounters in the background of this book is oddly grim and unpleasant: among the previously known types of pessimism, none seems to have reached this degree of malignancy. This lack of contrast between true and apparent world: there is only one world, and this is wrong, cruel, contradictory, seductive, with no sense... is a world so constituted the real world... We have a lie necessary to this reality, this "truth" to come to the victory that is to live a lie... That is necessary in order to live, which is even with this terrible and questionable character of existence...

The metaphysics, morality, religion, science - they are in this book simply as different forms of deceit considered: with their aid is believed to life. "Life should inspire confidence": the task, so placed, is immense. To solve it, a person must already be a liar by nature, he must be more than any other artist... And yet he is also: Metaphysics, morality, religion, science - all just figments of his will to art, to lie, to escape from the "truth", to deny the "truth". This property itself, thanks to which he rapes reality with the lie, this artist-asset par excellence of man - he still has it with everything that is in common: he himself is indeed a piece of reality, truth, nature - it is even also a piece of genius lies...

That the character of existence is ignored - lowest and highest secret intention science, religion, artistic community. See much never see much wrong, much to see...

Oh, how wise is still, in states where it is farthest away from that, to think wisely! The love, the enthusiasm, "God" - all subtleties of the last self-deception, all seductions to life! In moments when humans become the dupes, which he believes to life again, where he has outsmarted themselves: oh, how it swells up as him! What a delight! What feeling of power! How much artistic triumph in the sense of power!... The man was once again master of the "stuff" - masters of the truth!... And whenever a man is pleased, he is always the same in his joy, he is happy as an artist, he enjoys himself as a power. The lie is the power...

The art and nothing but the art. It is the great facilitator of life, the great seducer to life the great stimulus to life...

11 [416]

Revaluation of values.

Book 1: the Antichrist.

Book 2: the Misosoph.

Book 3: the Immoralist Book

4: Dionysus.

Revaluation of all values.

11[417]

I have the Germans <Translator: one letter "D" in the text for Deutschen likely> the most profound book given that they possess, my Zarathustra -1 give them now the most independent. How? I said to my conscience, as you like throwing pearls before the Germans!...

(ich habe den D das tiefste Buch gegeben, das sie besitzen, meinen Zarathustra — ich gebe ihnen heute das unabhangigste. Wie? sagt mir dazu mein schlechtes Gewissen, wie willst du Perlen vor die Deutschen werfen!...)